T

SECOND CHANCE

Stella Gioacas

MAPLE
PUBLISHERS

Their Second Chance

Author: Stella Gioacas

First Published in 2021

ISBN 978-1-915164-23-0 (Paperback)
978-1-915164-22-3 (Ebook)

Published by:
Maple Publishers
1 Brunel Way,
Slough,
SL1 1FQ, UK
www.maplepublishers.com

Cover Design and Book Layout by:
White Magic Studios
www.whitemagicstudios.co.uk

A CIP catalogue record for this title is available from the British Library.

CONTENTS

Chapter 1

Sophie was sitting in the front aisle of the church, as usual, waiting for the service to begin.

She had always found the church a calming place to be in, the dim lights, the smell of beeswax and incense, the flickering candle flames which she always found mesmerizing, and would often find herself lost, staring into the naked flames until something or someone would pull her back to reality.

Beside her sat Maria, an elderly woman who never missed a Sunday service, and whom Sophie had grown quite fond of over the last five years since she started attending church on a regular basis.

Maria leaned over to whisper in Sophie's ear that she had heard a rumour that a new priest had been assigned to the church and that he would be conducting the service that day.

"I heard he's incredibly young, only thirty years old, apparently," she said to Sophie. "I just hope he's better than the last one we had," Maria finished as another woman who always sat on the bench just behind them leaned forward and whispered, "I heard he's not married, what a shame." "Why is that a shame?" Sophie asked, not one to join in on gossip in church but was curious after that remark.

"Kourimou, a man who is not married and chooses to become a priest can no longer marry," Maria explained.

"That's why they tend to wait until they marry before taking their second vows," the other woman finished. "If I was only fifty years younger..."

"Don't finish that sentence," Maria said to her while doing the sign of the cross.

Sophie stifled a giggle thinking the 'shame' remark now made a lot of sense.

Sophie was very fond of the two women and found their little conversations very funny. Both women reminded her so much of her mother. She missed her mother dearly. It had been six years since she last saw her, maybe one day she will see her again. They often spoke on the phone, but it will never be the same as seeing her and holding her, because no matter how old you are you will always want and need your mother.

She blamed her father for how things had turned out and most of all she blamed Stefano!

She would never forget the day she had lost everything and everyone she cared about, and she would never forgive. Pretty ironic how she came to church every week asking for forgiveness but could not give that same forgiveness back, she thought to herself.

She found herself remembering the past, the day she went to see Stefano at his father's villa back home in Cyprus. The day she wanted to tell him that she was pregnant and all about the conversation she had had with her father and the ultimatum he had given her, "It's him and that baby or us."

She wanted to tell him that she picked him and their baby and they were going to be a family, just like they always spoke about. She wanted to be held in his strong arms, arms that always made her feel protected and safe, to be told that everything would be ok, and her father would come round in the end but instead it was another man who opened the door that day. He might have looked like her Stefano, but he certainly did not behave like her Stefano, this man was cruel!

She would always remember the look of pure hatred on his face when he told her he hated her and never wanted to see her again, all the ugly names he had called her, a whore, a witch- words she would never forget.

She then made her way back home feeling used, broken, humiliated and found her father standing in the open doorway with her mother standing behind him, her eyes red rimmed and puffy from crying. The smirk on her father's face telling her he somehow knew she would be coming back. As she tried to step past him into the house he blocked her way, stinking of alcohol as always. "Have you decided what you are going to do girly?" he asked her and without any doubt, with her head held high, she replied, "I'm keeping my baby."

He bent down, taking a bag which she did not notice earlier and tossing it to her, said, "You're on your own."

She would never forget the sound of her mother crying as she walked away, the look of contempt on her father's face. She would often relive those awful moments in her sleep, her mother's cries, the twisted look on Stefano's face as he called her a whore.

Sophie brought her mind sharply back to the present as the church bell finally rang out, signaling the service was about to begin and as the priest came out looking straight ahead, Sophie froze.

Stefano! Sophie's heart skipped a beat.

But no, not Stefano. For a split second she actually thought the new priest was Stefano, he was the spitting image of the man.

She concentrated on his face as he began the service, quietly playing 'spot the difference' in her mind. The hair was the same - black, cut short, neat, almost square like. His lips were the same, just the right amount of generous, not too big, and not too small and the same square jaw.

But when she looked up to his eyes, she spotted her first difference. This man might look like Stefano, but their eyes were nothing alike; where Stefano's eyes were deep and dark, this man's were light and bright, like day and night, heaven and hell she thought - It was a good thing this guy was on the bright side considering he was a priest.

Suddenly she sensed a movement on her right; somebody arriving late and hurrying to get a seat. She turned her head to smile at whoever it was and Sophie's whole world came crashing down.

Sophie's heart gave a painful thump in her chest as she found herself face to face with the man himself - Stefano!

And this wasn't a case of mistaken identity, it was really him! Standing tall in a black, tailored suit and white shirt, looking down at her.

Suddenly, she felt very hot and sick, her breathing felt restricted, her chest felt heavy, her stomach churning. This cannot be real, Sophie was thinking. How could he be here? Why is he in London? Of all the places on earth, he had to turn up here, in this very church!

The last time she saw him was in Cyprus.

She wanted to run away from him like she did six years ago but she felt rooted to the spot. Her legs felt like jelly, and she honestly thought she was going to be sick right here in the church.

Did he know she was here? Did her mother tell him she was here? Was he here for Christina?

With all these questions firing in her head, she forced herself to look straight ahead.

Glancing at the side door on her right which was only a few feet away from her, she wanted to bolt out of it and keep running until she got as far away from here as possible. But there were two problems with that plan. One was that Stefano was standing right beside her blocking her way and two, nobody came to church just to run out as the service began and Sophie knew how much they all loved to gossip here. Sometimes it felt more like a social club rather than a church.

Plus, she knew that if she suddenly walked out, Maria would be worried and bound to start ringing her and what would she say to the old woman. And not to mention that, this was also Christina's Saturday school.

So, she decided that she would stick it out, keep her head down and as soon as the service was over, she would make her escape. Thank God, Christina isn't here, she thought. That wouldn't have made it more awkward at all, she thought, sarcastically.

Halfway through the service she risked a sideways glance in his direction and caught him watching her with those impenetrable eyes of his, the same eyes that had always felt like they could see deep into her soul. Looking quickly away, heart beating painfully fast, Sophie flicked out her tongue to try and moisten her suddenly dry lips but instead realized she had no moisture left as her mouth and throat felt bone dry.

In the end she didn't know which way to turn and look; she had Stefano on her right, staring daggers at her and up in front was the priest who of all people looked the spitting image of Stefano. Suddenly an idea popped into her head - were they related? She knew he had a younger half-brother, one she didn't get to meet as he lived in Greece with his mother, was that him? It would certainly explain the resemblance.

As the service finally ended Sophie picked up her bag and after saying a quick goodbye to Maria she walked past the old woman and around the bench to head towards the door rather than squeeze by Stefano. She was so close to the door on her way out when Elena, Christina's teacher, was coming in through that very door and stopped Sophie in her tracks.

"Ah, Sophia mou, I'm glad I bumped into you. Are you still happy to help out next Saturday with the bake sale?"

The church committee was holding a bake sale where all the proceeds were going towards fixing the church roof which was in urgent need of repair and Elena was in charge of organizing the event in which Sophie had agreed to help and do some baking. "I'm not too sure, something has come up and I'm not sure if I can anymore. I will let you know. I'm sorry I have to go." And she practically ran out the door like the hounds of hell were at her heels, almost knocking Elena down.

Stefano remained standing where he was as he watched the brief exchange between Sophie and Elena.

From where he was standing, they seemed to already know each other, not to mention he also caught the way she said goodbye to the elderly woman on his left and how she tenderly gave the woman's hand a little squeeze. It was obvious that Sophie was well known here, so it was safe to assume that this was her local church, meaning that she couldn't be living too far from here. But what wasn't clear was, why she was here. He never knew her to be the religious type. Maybe she wanted forgiveness for what she did, he thought bitterly. Well, God could forgive her, but he certainly wouldn't.

Of all the places, he had to bump into her here, now. He was only planning on being here in London for a few days as he had promised Luke, his brother that he would be there for him for moral support as he settled into his new life here at the church. Luke had only taken his vows last week in Cyprus and the archbishop had already assigned him to a church and much to Luke's surprise, he was to learn it was in London. Stefano had the sneaky suspicion that it wasn't a very pleasant surprise so had decided to come along which his brother unsurprisingly did not object to.

A few more days and he'd be gone, hopefully he wouldn't see her again.

He had to admit, he was curious, though, curious about how and why she was even here in London. From what he knew all her family was back in Cyprus, who did she know here?

Seeing Sophie again after all these years deeply unsettled him and he didn't like the feeling.

He had loved her once, cherished her and she had twisted that love and turned it into a hate that burned so fiercely in his heart that it was ingrained deep in his soul.

His brother would say that hate is the devil's path, but he would happily walk that path.

She had betrayed him, lied to him, led him to believe she felt the same way, wanted the same things but when she fell pregnant the truth came out.

She didn't even have the decency to tell him about the abortion herself. Oh no, her father had that pleasure! Coming to his house and telling him that his bastard child was dead. Christ! He didn't even know that she was pregnant in the first place, running a hand through his hair at the memory. Of course, he didn't believe him at first, the whole village knew him to be a crazy drunk but when he called Sophie and she didn't pick up, he called her mother and she confirmed that what her husband said was true.

That day was the day the seed of hate was planted in his heart and he promised himself he would never be fooled by a woman again! And that was the day his nightmare began.

Even after all these years, the nightmare was always the same. He would find himself in a crowded street, on a dark rainy day with people all around him. He's walking down the street with his hand outstretched and in the palm of his hand is a very tiny baby. In the dream he is desperately trying to find the baby's mother, but everybody just walks past him like he is invisible, then he looks down and realizes that the baby is dead. That's the point when he wakes up, heart frantically beating and sweating from head to foot.

She had condemned him to this nightmare, and he would always hate her for it.

Seeing Elena coming towards him he put on a smile. He and Luke had met her yesterday when she showed them around the church and the school next door which she was in charge of running. She seemed nice enough but how well did you know someone after just one meeting? Trust didn't seem to come so easily to him anymore especially where women were considered.

"Yasou Stefano, how did the service go? Luke seemed very nervous this morning."

"It went very well, thank you. Luke was born for the church."

"Oh, I'm glad. I'm just sorry I missed it. I was stuck in the office all morning trying to organize this bake sale we're having next week and now it seems that my best baker might be pulling out."

On hearing the 'best baker' part he instantly knew that she was talking about Sophie. Cooking was always her passion and once upon a time in another life he had intended buying her, her very own restaurant as a wedding gift.

But hey, shit happens.

"Was that the lady you were speaking with, by the door, earlier?" he found himself asking.

"Yes, that's Sophia. I promise you, if you have just one of her sugar-coated cookies, you will be an addict for life," Elena replied, full of pride as if she was talking about her own cooking.

"You seem to know her very well, has she been attending here long?" He asked the question before it even formed in his mind; just curiosity, he told himself.

"Yes, well, she's been coming here for the past five years now, and her daughter is in my class. Lovely girls, both of them, although I don't seem to know that much about her, to be honest. She seems to keep herself to herself most of the time."

Stefano felt himself going cold at the mention of 'her daughter'.

He had to ask, "How old is her daughter?"

"She's going to be five soon, in a few months."

At that point an elderly lady came over wanting to speak to Elena giving him the perfect chance to excuse himself, and walk outside into the courtyard at the back, desperately needing the fresh air. Sophie had a child!

He couldn't believe what he had just heard. He clenched his hands into fists. He hadn't been this angry in a very long time. The last time had again been with Sophie. That woman just seemed to bring out the worst in him!

After doing some quick calculations, from the girl's age it seemed that Sophie got pregnant right after. Why abort his child and not the next one? And who was the father? And what made that man any better than him? A thought suddenly occurred to him. Was she with this other man when she was with him? Did she cheat on him? Or did she simply just move on from one bed to the next?

He felt sick to his stomach at the thought of Sophie being with another man then coming back to him and his bed. He had once thought that they had something special, but he couldn't have been more wrong.

He would make her pay like he should have done years ago.

Chapter 2

Sophie finally made it through the front door of her tiny flat and instantly threw herself on the sofa.

What a day this was shaping up to be! The bus journey from the church was horrendous, her stomach felt so bad that she spent the entire journey sitting at the back of the bus with her hand over her mouth praying for the vomit that threatened to come up to stay down, at least until she got home.

But she was safe now; sitting down on the sofa she buried her face in her hands.

She couldn't stop thinking about Stefano, seeing him in the church this morning after all these years. She never in a million years thought she would see him again especially here where she lived, in this part of London; it just wasn't him.

During her pregnancy she often fantasied about bumping into him and Stefano telling her how much he loved her, that he shouldn't have let her go. But once Christina came along, that fantasy had died away. Her daughter was her world now and that man could rot in hell.

Though she knew she didn't actually mean that, because deep down she knew she still loved him, always had. He sliced her heart in two, destroyed her and at times when thinking of that dreadful day six years ago she would feel such anger that she believed she hated him. But then she would remember all the good times they had together, how in love she believed them to be at the time and the tears would start to flow. Someone once said in a movie although she couldn't remember for the life of her what movie it was now, but they said that true love never dies, and she hated to admit it, but Stefano was her one true love and always will be.

Sighing, she realized she still had her coat and shoes on when the doorbell suddenly rang. It must be Christina with Susan, she thought. Although, looking at her watch, she thought they were a couple of hours early. Christina enjoyed spending time with the woman who lived in the flat below them on the second floor.

Sophie really loved her too and had depended on her quite a bit in the early days when Christina was born. They had met on the stairwell a couple of days after a heavily pregnant Sophie moved in and she had been in the process of trying to push a baby cot - one of those silly self-assembly ones in a box up the stairs. Susan had helped her take it indoors and after a cup of tea as a way of Sophie saying thank you, ended up helping her put the cot together. It took them well over a couple of hours to do but that was the beginning of their friendship, the only friendship Sophie really had. So, when Christina was finally born Susan was always around with a helping hand, so naturally as Christina was growing up, they developed a natural bond. Now every Sunday when Sophie went to church, Christina would go downstairs to Susan's.

Kicking off her shoes, she stood up while taking off her coat and flinging it over the sofa, and went to open the door expecting to see Christina and Susan, instead she came face to face with Stefano! For the second time that day.

Standing tall and straight, still dressed in his Sunday best, he still looked like he did six years ago, stunning!

"Stefano!" Sophie's heart gave a painful thump in her chest. If this continued, she was afraid she might have a heart attack.

"Sophie," he nodded. "May I come in?" it was a question but without waiting for an answer he simply walked past her and into her small hallway.

Why bother asking? She thought to herself but didn't dare say anything out loud.

"Is your husband home?" he asked, looking around.

Husband? Maybe she should say 'yes', or would he know she was lying. "Erm yes, no," Sophie responded with a shake of her head. Omg, what was she thinking, well she wasn't thinking. Obviously, she had to get it together and quick, don't look like a fool in front of him.

But one look at him told her she was too late on the whole not looking like a fool bit.

"Yes, no? What are you not sure of?" Stefano asked with a raised eyebrow. He would have found it amusing under different circumstances, she never was a good liar. How could anybody live here, he thought, looking around the tiny flat, especially with a kid, but who cares, it wasn't his kid. From where he was standing, he could see the whole place, the open plan living/kitchen area on his left, the little bathroom just behind him and the bedroom on his right. Clearly, they were alone.

"I meant 'no', but he'll be home soon." Looking down at her feet, Sophie was not surprised to find that her voice sounded shaky as by now her whole body was trembling and her heart was racing like a horse on a racetrack. Her stomach was also doing somersaults again.

How did he know where she lived? He couldn't have followed her here because she got the bus, and he certainly wasn't on it! But more importantly why was he here? It couldn't possibly be for Christina because he didn't give a damn six years ago so why would he now?

Swallowing down the bile that creeped up her throat, she looked up and saw that he was smirking. Oh, he was enjoying this for sure.

"What?" she asked, a little too sharply.

"Don't what me." Suddenly his tone changed. He knew she was lying because when he had looked up her address that morning on the school records which were held in his brother's office, he noticed the church had her down as a Miss and not a Mrs. Not to mention the fact that every time she lied, she always looked down, must be her guilty conscience, he thought. But this woman had told one too many lies.

"You're a liar." He gritted out; he was so close to losing his temper. He liked to think of himself as a calm man but not when it came to Sophie. Just thinking about her had his blood boiling and admittedly not always with anger.

Sophie was stunned! Stunned that he would even call her a liar in the first place but also because he said it with such fierce hatred that it felt like a slap in the face.

"Why would you say something like that? What have I ever done to you?" Instinctively, she crossed her arms across her body and that's when she felt her chin begin to tremble, tears begin to well up and she tried desperately to fight them down, not wanting to show any weakness.

"Oh, don't play the victim with me, Sophie, because we both know you're not! Just as we both know there is no husband, so cut the crap!"

Sophie just continued to stare at him, she didn't understand what was happening here.

But she needed to know why he was here.

"How did you find out where I live? Did you follow me?" she asked.

"The church," flicking his hand as if to imply it was nothing.

"They wouldn't just give you my address." Well, she hoped not, otherwise she'll be filing a complaint.

"I never said they did."

Sophie was beginning to get frustrated; she should have known she wouldn't get a straight answer out of him.

Taking a deep breath, she asked again, "Then how did you find out where I live?"

"I told you the church..."

When he saw Sophie open her mouth about to say something, "Oh, keep your dirty little panties on! I got your address from the school records in the office."

Sophie's heart felt like it dislodged from its central location and fell right through into her stomach.

The school records, that must mean he knows about Christina. Fear suddenly fluttered in her stomach, that must be why he was here. What if he wanted to take her little girl away from her?

What scared her the most was the fact that she knew he could. He had money backing him up, while she had nothing. He could offer Christina so much more than she ever could, but at the end of the day he would never be able to give her what she truly needed and that was love. Because the man had no heart, no soul.

She suddenly became conscience of the fact that Christina was only downstairs and could come up at any time, panic now rising in her she realized she had to get him out of here as quickly as possible.

Sophie never spoke to Christina about her father, and she never asked either but then again, she wasn't at that age yet to start wondering why she didn't have a daddy like her friends. She often thought long and hard about what she would say when the time came and Christina would finally bring up the subject, she never did think of an answer. Should she be honest and tell her the cold hard truth, that her father never wanted them? No, she couldn't and wouldn't do that to her! But she would cross that bridge when she got to it, and she was determined that today was not the day.

"Listen, Stefano, I have things I need to get on with, what is it you want?"

"You trying to get rid of me, Sophie? Will your fictional husband come home and catch me here?" raising his eyebrows, daring her to lie to him again.

He was seething with anger, who the hell did she think she was?

He could see that she was nervous, possibly even afraid and that gave him a deep sense of satisfaction. She should be afraid, he thought, he was going to make her pay for what she did.

He took a couple of steps forward and she instinctively took a couple back, then there was nowhere left to go. With her back against the wall, she wrapped her arms round herself even tighter.

She had never been afraid of him in the past, but she found that she was afraid of him now. He wasn't the same man she remembered and when she looked up into his eyes, she saw an almost violent anger that was barely controlled.

He wouldn't harm her, would he? She thought. Well, this certainly wasn't the man she used to know and love that was for sure. What happened to him, to make him change so much?

One day they were happy and planning their future and the next he kicked her to the curb, just like that.

"Look, I don't even care what you want any more, Stefano, I think you should just leave, or I'll call the police. As far as I'm concerned, we have nothing to say to each other."

Smirking, Stefano took another step towards her. He was now so close he swore he could smell the fear rolling off her as well as feel her hot sweet breath on his face.

Anger swept through him, although that anger wasn't for her but more for himself; even after everything she had done, one look at her and he found himself wishing he could touch her, hold her. Pushing it back down, hands clenching by his sides, he suddenly grabbed her by her wrist, maybe a little harder than he intended but certainly not as hard as he wanted. Bringing his face up close and looking her straight in the eyes, "You threaten to call the police on me, yet you're the one who got away with murder."

The way he said those words, quietly and calmly made goosebumps rise on her skin.

Murder? What was he talking about? Was he having some sort of mental breakdown? She didn't remember him having any mental health problems when they were together but then again, men rarely speak about that sort of stuff, even in this day and age.

His hand locked around her wrist made her nervous. It wasn't as much painful as it was uncomfortable, but she could feel the barely controlled strength behind it, if he wanted, he could easily snap her wrist in half.

She had to get him to calm down and out the door as quickly as possible, she definitely didn't want him around when Christina came up.

"Stefano, let's just calm down, I don't know what you're..."

He didn't give her the chance to finish - to finish what exactly, more lies?

God, the woman never stopped, he wanted to throttle her!

She had no idea how close he was to losing control.

"Don't give me that. Don't act like you don't know what I'm talking about," he said bitterly.

"I honestly don't," she said in a whisper, she was so close to crying now.

"Again, with the lies Sophie, WHEN will you stop!" he said louder this time and giving her wrist a tighter squeeze. "I know all about the abortion." Seeing her stunned face, he went on, "Yeah that's right, what? Did you think I would never find out?"

Abortion? What abortion? To say she was confused was a huge understatement.

She could feel her heart beating rapidly, her hands were beginning to tingle, and the room was beginning to spin. She could see hundreds of tiny white dots all over and around Stefano's face.

Thank God she was standing with her back against the wall as she could feel herself sliding down the wall.

Stefano let go off her wrist and moved back, slowly and uncertainly. What was wrong with her? He could tell she wasn't faking it as he saw the moment her face completely drained of color, the unfocused look in her eyes.

Maybe he pushed her too far, he thought. But he hadn't even started! He wanted her to know that he knew, to unsettle her, even frighten her a bit if he was completely honest with himself.

And he expected a reaction, he expected her to deny it, to yell and swear, maybe even give him a slap pretending to be insulted. But he didn't expect this, he thought as he watched her ashen face, something was wrong here.

Kneeling in front of her he put a hand on her shoulder. He could feel her body trembling. "Sophie, what's wrong?"

She looked like she was hyperventilating.

"Take deep slow breaths and maybe put your head between your knees."

Sophie was shaking her head, her vision was disfigured making her feel sick, there seemed to be three Stefanos each swaying from side to side. Oh god, please don't let me die, she silently prayed. She held on to a mental image of Christina as she tried to focus on her breathing.

"It's just a panic attack, come on, you'll be fine. Deep slow breaths." He said again.

But Sophie was shaking her head, trying to speak.

"No...my bag...get...my bag." She managed to get out as she was gasping for breath.

"Where's your bag?" now he was starting to panic. He had never seen anyone having a panic attack before and certainly never Sophie in all the years he knew her. But he noticed the way she was clutching at her chest, and it didn't seem in line with a panic attack.

"Sofa."

He jumped on his feet and in five long strides was in the living room. He grabbed her oversized bag off the sofa and was back kneeling in front of her with super-fast speed.

Handing her the bag he saw her reach in and retrieve a little pill packet, with trembling hands she opened the little box and popped out a tiny red pill.

"Water...please."

Without a word, he quickly went to the tiny kitchen and thankfully found a glass in the first cupboard he looked in and filled it with water. Rushing back to her, he handed it over, keeping his hand near the glass while she was drinking in case she dropped it as he could see her hands were still shaking.

What were these pills for, that she was taking? He decided to wait until whatever this episode was, to finish before he asked any questions.

Setting the glass down by her side, they both sat there in silence for a while.

Sophie, resting her head on her drawn-up knees, taking deep slow breaths and Stefano by her side with his back against the wall quietly watching her and thanking all the gods when he saw her breathing had returned to normal.

This was not going down as he expected; she certainly had a lot of explaining to do.

After a while when she was feeling a bit more like herself, still shaky but better, she realized that he was sitting patiently beside her. He didn't leave her; that realization alone had her baffled.

While her head was on her knees she decided to take this opportunity to think about everything that had just happened. What he said earlier, then the sudden change in character after she had one of her attacks. In all honesty, when he let go off her wrist and she slid down to the floor, she thought he was going to walk away and just leave her there on the floor. But he didn't, he stayed and helped and for that she was thankful.

Slowly lifting her head and turning towards him she saw him watching her. His face didn't betray any emotions, so she had no idea what he was thinking, but at least he wasn't ranting and raving like a madman anymore.

She was however grateful for his help just now. God only knows what would have happened if he wasn't here but on the other hand she thought, this probably wouldn't have happened if he wasn't here.

"Thank you." Well, she did owe him that.

"I didn't do anything." He found that his voice was surprisingly tender when he spoke. He had thought he despised her, wanted to hurt her the same way she hurt him but not physically. Never physically.

But that wasn't a simple panic attack like he originally thought, something else was wrong.

He suddenly had an overwhelming need to know. He shouldn't, he told himself. Just get up off the damn floor and walk out that door which he noticed was still wide open.

He stood up with every intention of doing that but found himself closing the door instead.

Just curiosity, he told himself, don't overthink it.

Turning back towards her, he extended his hand, "Come on, let's get you off the floor."

Sophie's gaze travelled from his hand to his face, and she saw something in his eyes which she wasn't quite sure of. She wasn't sure of anything anymore, but it certainly wasn't anger, it was replaced by something much more tender.

Taking her hand, he helped her to her feet, "Let's get you to the kitchen and get a coffee down you, it will do you good." With the floor still moving beneath her feet and with Stefano guiding her by the elbow, she slowly made her way to the kitchen and took a seat at the little folding table she had at the far end by the balcony.

"Thank you." She found herself saying again for the second time within minutes. One minute he was yelling at her, accusing her of God knows what and the next she's thanking him, going from one extreme to the next.

"Where do you keep the coffee?" he asked, looking around the tiny kitchen.

"The cupboard next to the fridge."

It wasn't a big kitchen, and the fridge was just on his right, practically touching his shoulder, he felt like a giant in this place.

On opening the cupboard, he found some instant decaff, what the hell was this shit? The Sophie he remembered, liked her coffee strong.

Pulling a face, he turned back around and saw that she had her elbows on the table and was resting her head in her hands.

"You ok?" he asked.

"Yeah, I'll be fine soon."

"Do you have any of the Greek stuff?" he asked holding up the jar of decaff.

"No, sorry. Only decaff."

It will have to do, he thought.

Putting on the kettle and opening another cupboard, he found it almost bare apart from a few cans of tuna and chopped tomatoes. Opening yet another cupboard, he found what he was looking for and took down two mugs.

On opening the fridge, he found that to be almost bare, too. Apart from the milk he was looking for, there were only a few items such as fresh pasta, cheese and ham. Well, no wonder she almost collapsed! Did she have some sort of eating disorder?

But what about the kid, what was she feeding her? Again, don't even wonder about the kid, it's not your problem, he told himself, giving his head a shake as if to clear the unwanted thoughts.

Having made the coffee, he took the two mugs to the table and took the only other seat opposite her.

"I put a couple of spoons of sugar in there, it will help," he said when he noticed her hands were still shaky when she reached out and took her mug.

"Thank you." Third time, she thought.

She couldn't hold it in anymore, she had to ask. He was acting like someone who cared, he could fool a million people, but he couldn't fool her.

"Why are you suddenly being so nice to me? Just a few minutes ago you were yelling and practically manhandling me and now you're making me coffee!"

"First, I wasn't manhandling you, let's get that straight. And second, what did you expect me to do, let you pass out?" taking a sip of his coffee and pulling a face, god this was disgusting.

"No, of course not." Taking a sip of her coffee and looking up at him over her mug she whispered, "thank you." Fourth time!

"You can stop thanking me and tell me what actually happened just now because I'm no expert but that didn't seem like a simple panic attack to me."

"I just forgot to take my pill this morning, that's all, it's nothing. I'll be fine."

"What pill? And that didn't look like nothing to me." So, something was wrong. But what bothered him the most right this second was why he was even asking. Just walk away, he told himself again. She's sitting down, you made her coffee, you've done your duty, now go.

Putting her coffee down and cradling the hot mug between her hands, "Look, I really appreciate you helping me earlier, but I really don't think it's any of your business."

"It is my business when you collapse right in front of me."

"I didn't collapse, don't exaggerate. I just felt a little dizzy, that's all."

She always was a terrible liar, she was hiding something. "That was more than just a dizzy spell and we both know it."

The man was like a dog with a bone, relentlessly stubborn when he wanted to be.

Maybe she should just tell him and stop being childish, it wasn't like it was a secret or anything, maybe when his curiosity was satisfied, he would then leave.

"I have a heart condition. Nothing serious but it causes an irregular and fast beat, really catches my breath when that happens."

"Since when?" he blurted out, a little too harshly, but he was completely baffled. She never mentioned a heart condition before, he would have remembered something like that. He remembered everything about her, including how she liked her damn coffee! They were together for five years, damn it! Did he ever actually know this woman?

Sophie didn't like his tone of voice. Was he trying to imply that she was lying? Why would she?

With her head held high and looking him straight in the eyes, she said, "Since I had Christina."

Seeing him narrow his eyes in confusion, she continued, well no point in stopping now, might as well go all the way. He wanted to know, so be it.

"It's called Wolff-Parkinson-White syndrome. Apparently, I was born with it. It just never caused me any issues before."

She was feeling the need to make him feel bad, if that was even possible with him. She had gone through hell and back to have her daughter and she had gone through it alone. Now he was sitting opposite her, all high and mighty asking her 'since when?'

How dare he?

"Pregnancy puts a lot of pressure on the heart, you know. And having my daughter made the condition worse."

Oh, she was really twisting that knife in, wasn't she? he thought. Reminding him that she had another man's kid.

Anger was spreading quickly through every nerve in his body. Getting up he walked over to the sink and poured his coffee down the drain. That was bad coffee and he needed to control his temper.

"Yes, your daughter," he said bitterly with his back to her.

If she wasn't afraid of falling over right now, she would have got up and punched him right in the nose.

"Yes, our daughter!"

Chapter 3

Stefano froze!

Did she just say what he thought she said or was his mind playing cruel tricks on him?

"What did you say?" he slowly turned around and walked back to the table facing her. Planting both hands on the table, he looked her straight in the eyes. "What did you just say?" he repeated when she just stared back at him.

Fury was radiating off him, just like those electric heaters that radiated heat to the person standing directly in front of them, she thought.

Should she repeat herself or stay quiet and try to calm the situation in some way?

For the first time since he walked through her door, she found herself silently praying that Susan and Christina would come up.

"I said, what did you say?" What did she mean by that, she had to explain, damn it.

Banging his fist on the table when she didn't respond, he was in danger of losing control.

Sophie nearly jumped out of her skin, swallowing hard, voice barely a whisper, "I said, our daughter."

Cocking his head to the side, "Now why would you go and say something like that when we both know she's not mine. You are one seriously twisted woman." He finished through gritted teeth.

Turning around and walking over to the balcony door, looking out, he sucked in a deep breath. He felt like he'd just been punched in the gut. Only God knew how much he wanted that statement to be true.

Watching him standing there with his back to her, she was close to tears now. She was exhausted, both mentally and physically by his ever-changing mood swings. He was being just like Dr. Jekyll and Mr. Hyde.

"Why would YOU say something like that? Of course, she's yours. What exactly are you accusing me of? Cheating on you? Because for the record, I didn't, and where the hell would you get an idea like that from?"

Tears were welling up now and threatening to spill over. It felt like her heart was breaking all over again, not that it actually mended in the first place.

"Well, it certainly would explain how you moved on so quickly." Turning around to face her now, "And I know about the abortion Sophie, so you can stop pretending." He said, he was beginning to get a sour taste in his mouth. "And I also know how old your daughter is, I did the math Sophie, do you think I'm that stupid?"

Abortion? How did he come up with that one? She nearly laughed out loud but managed to hold it in, that would have been like throwing petrol on an open fire.

Did he expect her to have an abortion when he broke up with her? Is that why he was so angry? That would explain a lot, maybe he thought she would ask for child support, the bastard was probably worried about his money.

Well, he didn't need to worry, if she wanted anything from him, she would have asked for it by now, but she didn't. She didn't want a single penny from him. She had gotten by so far and she would continue to do so.

"I very obviously didn't have an abortion!"

The impact of those words had knocked the air out of his lungs. His eyebrows came together, "but I thought..."

"You thought what? That I would abort my own baby just because you were a coward? And just for the record, if it's your money you're so worried about, then don't be, I don't want a single penny from you."

Coward? He wasn't a coward! He wanted that baby, wanted her, them. Was it possible she was telling the truth?

"You're lying," he said, but without much conviction this time.

"No. I'm not."

His legs felt like lead. Pulling out a chair, he sat back down at the table. Shaking his head in disbelief, "But he said..."

"Who said?"

"Your father."

"My father said what? What's he got to do with any of this?"

This was beginning to grate on her nerves.

"That day, the last time I saw you..."

"The day you broke up with me." How could she forget?

He hated thinking about that day, it sliced through his heart like a knife. Pinching the bridge of his nose and releasing a slow controlled breath, he continued,

"Yes, that day your father came to see me. Drunk as usual, ranting, and raving about our relationship, the business, my father..."

"Nothing new there then." She thought sourly.

"But then he said you had an abortion! In his own words ..." using his fingers to quote "you aborted my bastard child."

"And you believed him?" Thunderstruck, she couldn't believe what she was hearing. How could her father stoop so low!

"No, of course not. Not at first anyway. But when I called you and you didn't pick up, I then called your mother. She confirmed what your father said to be true."

"What?" she was beginning to get dizzy again.

If what he was saying was true.... God, she couldn't even think it in her head. How could her father do something like that?

Stefano missing the early years of Christina's life, first steps, first words. Not to mention all the heartache and everything she went through for that matter, with the pregnancy and delivery and everything she was still going through, all because of a bitter old man.

Suddenly the doorbell rang, startling them both out of their thoughts. Looking at her watch, she realized it was Christina and Susan.

They both stood up and Stefano, looking past her into the hallway, he asked, "Is that her?"

Her heart leapt into her throat - what if he suddenly blurted it out to Christina that he was her father? Obviously, the truth had to come out eventually, but it had to be handled with care.

Not to mention she still didn't fully understand everything that happened, they still had a lot to talk about, but now was not the time.

"Yes, but please don't say anything, Stefano. Not yet, we need to talk first."

There was a moment's silence in which he just stared into the hallway, not speaking, the doorbell ringing out again.

"Stefano? Please." This was traumatizing enough as it was, she didn't want Christina traumatized as well.

Looking back at her and seeing the desperate pleading in her eyes, he nodded, "Ok, I won't. But we do need to talk. Tonight. I'll send a car to pick you up at seven."

Letting out a breath she didn't realise she was holding in, she walked towards the door but before opening the door she turned back round and mouthed a silent "thank you."

After a late lunch of fish and chips which over the years became their Sunday tradition, the three of them settled down in front of the television and were watching Christina's favorite DVD.

Halfway through the movie Sophie went to get a drink, motioning for Susan to follow. Once in the kitchen and out of ear shot, Sophie asked if Susan could have Christina for the night.

Stefano said he would pick her up at seven and God knew what time she would be back. Besides when she got back, all she would probably want to do is crawl under the duvet and cry herself to sleep. Thank God she had Susan.

"Sure sweetie, no problem." Leaning in closer to whisper, "Is it to do with that guy who was here earlier? Because I could taste the static in the air when I walked in."

Looking over her shoulder and seeing that Christina was still engrossed in her movie, she whispered back, "Yeah, that was Stefano."

"Thee Stefano?" raising her eyebrows.

Of course, Susan knew all about Stefano and her past.

"Yeah, thee Stefano."

After the movie and after giving her mum a big kiss and cuddle, Christina and Susan went back downstairs, promising to call if there were any problems. She knew Christina was in safe hands, she wouldn't have left her with anybody else.

After a quick shower she dressed simply in black skinny jeans and a black blouse. She looked like a cat burglar, she thought, looking at herself in the mirror.

Deep down she knew she was trying to look good. Secretly she wanted him to think she was still attractive. Since having Christina, no matter how much she tried, she just couldn't shift those extra pounds, it was definitely harder the older you got. But she couldn't afford to think that way, not tonight; this wasn't going to be a social visit or a date for that matter. And why she should even feel that way, she had no idea. She was obviously losing her marbles and needed help.

And she shouldn't forget how cruel he could be, remember how he dumped you and all the vile things he said to you six years ago, she told her reflection.

As she looked at her watch and saw that it was seven, the doorbell rang, bang on time, she thought. He always did have an obsession with time, you couldn't even be a second late with that man.

On opening the door, she saw that it wasn't Stefano but a tall, young, handsome man who explained that he was sent by Mr. Christodoulou to take her to the hotel.

Sounds about right, she thought. Stefano always did like to make an impression. Picking up her bag and keys she closed her door and walked downstairs to the waiting car.

Stefano looked down at his watch, it was nearly eight o'clock, she should have been here by now, had she changed her mind? Or maybe they simply just found some traffic along the way. Pacing up and down in front of the vast windows of the penthouse, looking down at the ant-like people in the street below, he should feel like a king; he could have anything or anyone he wanted. But right now, he felt completely helpless, insecure, and most of all, alone. He hadn't felt this way in a very long time and he hated this feeling.

He was very aware that in the situation that they had found themselves in, Sophie held all the cards. But that was the point of this meeting, they had to talk about the past, get a few things straight and try to find a way to move forward. For both their sakes and especially for that little girl he didn't know existed, until today.

He knew the girl was his, he could feel it in his bones, but he still planned on asking for a DNA test because 'what if,' he thought. It was after all her own parents who told him she had an abortion - who could really blame him for being so conflicted?

Suddenly the phone on the console table rang, picking it up, "Hello?"

"Good evening Mr. Christodoulou, there's a Sophie Georgiou here to see you..."

"Send her up, thank you."

Putting down the phone, he blew out a long slow breath, she came.

Opening a bottle of red, he poured two glasses and placed them on the glass table in the living area. That was when he heard the knock on the door, it was her.

Opening the door and seeing her standing there in the open doorway, took his breath away. She had changed so much over the years it seemed and yet she was still the same. Seeing her again after all these years made him realize that maybe he didn't hate her as much as he thought he did. If what she was said was true, what then? Would it change anything between them, or had too much damage already been done?

"Hi, come in. Make yourself comfortable."

"Thank you," she said, feeling anything but comfortable and sadly doubted she would ever feel comfortable with this man again.

"Come, take a seat," gesturing towards the luxurious grey sofa in the middle of the room.

With Stefano leading the way, Sophie followed him over to the sofa and took a seat. He sat down next to her, not close enough to touch but close enough to give her those familiar butterflies she used to get whenever he was near.

Sitting here together on the sofa and seeing the wine on the table, the dim lights which gave the room a warm cozy glow, it all made her feel a little nervous. If the circumstances were different, she would have found all this romantic but right now she didn't know what she should feel or think.

Seeing him today made her realize how much he had changed; he wasn't the same man she used to know and love. The change wasn't physical, but there was a darkness around him now, which wasn't there before. She couldn't explain it, but it was something she could feel.

But that was why she was here against her better judgement, to talk, to find out what happened, what had changed!

Looking around, "Nice place, I guess the family business is doing well then."

"It is. I run it now, my father passed away four years ago, and my brother is in another line of work, as you know."

"Sorry about your father, he was a good man." And she really was, his father had been more of a father to her than her own father ever had.

"The best." He offered her a glass, "Drink?"

"Thank you." Taking it, she took a sip. What she really wanted to do however was to gulp it all down, just to calm her nerves of course, but managed to push that little urge down. It was good wine though; he always did have good taste in wine.

"I wasn't sure if you could drink, with your medication," picking up his own glass and taking a much bigger sip than she had, she noted.

He had already had quite a bit of brandy when he got back earlier and knew he shouldn't be mixing his drinks, but he also knew that Sophie wasn't one to drink alone. And he wanted her relaxed.

He deeply regretted the way in which he had handled the situation this afternoon, marching into her home all guns blazing, and what exactly did he achieve by that? Nothing!

This time he was planning on doing things differently.

"Everything in moderation is good for the heart, or so they say," she said, smiling. To hell with moderation she thought, she could easily down the whole bottle right now.

"Would you like something to eat? I could order something up."

"No, I'm fine, thank you."

Seeing his raised eyebrows she insisted, "Really, we had a late lunch and I'm still stuffed," she said, patting her tummy as if to prove a point.

Looking down and seeing her hand touch her tummy, he couldn't help noticing her breasts on the way up. Even though she had them covered under a black jumper, he could still see that they were rounder and much fuller than he remembered. She always had great breasts but motherhood it seemed had sculptured them to perfection. She never did need to wear tight or low-cut tops to emphasize her shape, in fact she had always done the opposite.

He was beginning to feel like a horny teenager, she always did have that effect on him. Even when he thought he hated her over the past six years, he would find himself thinking of the soft feel of her lips against his, the feel of her skin beneath his fingertips...

Feeling himself growing hard, he cleared his throat while pushing those thoughts to the side, "They have a fantastic chef, here, though not as good as you, obviously."

"Thank you for the compliment." Was he just looking at her breasts? She thought.

She felt her heart skip a beat, though not from her condition but from something else entirely different. This was a bad idea, she should have insisted they met up somewhere else, somewhere public but then again when she agreed to this meeting, she had no idea she was being brought here, she thought, looking around at her surroundings, anywhere but at Stefano.

Sensing she was beginning to feel uncomfortable, he decided to get straight to the point and stop beating around the bush. At the end of the day, they both knew why they were here.

"Where do we even begin?" he asked.

"Maybe you should start with what my father said to you, that seems to be the beginning of this whole nightmare, doesn't it?"

"It would seem," he said, taking a deep breath and blowing it out.

"Your father came round to see me that day," looking upwards and shaking his head at the memory. "I knew straight away that nothing good was going to come out of his visit as he was swaying from side to side and completely reeked of zivania."

"Yeah, his all-time favourite drink," she agreed bitterly. Remembering how her father was standing in the open doorway with a bottle of the stuff in his hand that day.

"He was very drunk that day," she added.

"That's an understatement! Anyway, like I said earlier, after ranting and raving about the usual, he then proceeded to tell me that you had an abortion. Imagine my surprise to learn that you were even pregnant."

"I was going to tell you, Stefano."

"What's done, is done now. Anyway, since we often spoke of marriage and children, naturally I didn't believe him."

Sophie took a sip of her wine; this was harder than she thought it would be.

"So, what went wrong? What changed your mind and you believed me to be such a monster that I would do something like that without even speaking to you first."

"After he left, I called you, Sophie, but you didn't answer..."

"Because I needed time to think, Stefano. Finding out I was pregnant came as a shock to me too."

"But I didn't know that at the time. Anyway, when you didn't answer, I called your mother to warn her that her husband was drunk again and was spouting some nonsense about you, that's when I realized she was crying. At first, I thought it was because she was worried about what her husband would do in his drunken state, but she ended up confirming what he had said to me."

Downing the rest of his wine in one gulp, he resisted the urge for a refill, he had to hold it together. He hated reliving that moment and he had relived it more times than he could count.

Sophie wasn't surprised with her mother. If she was completely honest with herself, her mother didn't have a mean bone in her body, but she was terrified of her husband, especially when he got drunk, which was often, if not daily, she thought to herself. She would have loved to have been angry with her, blame her for lying, for not sticking by her but she couldn't. She had managed to get away from that man, but her mother was still stuck with him.

"Did it ever occur to you that maybe he put her up to it? That maybe she was afraid not to do what she was told?" She didn't feel as much betrayed by her mother as she did by Stefano, he should have known better.

"No, it didn't." It had never occurred to him at the time that her mother might have lied out of fear; it should have, but he had allowed anger to cloud his judgment that day. If he could turn back time, he would.

"We were together for five years, Stefano, and we were friends for far longer. Like you said, we talked about marriage, children, the whole shebang, why would you just take their word and not speak to me first? You knew what my father was like." Unshed tears were beginning to burn the back of her throat, her voice was coming out like a croak. "You left me! I went through the pregnancy all alone, with no one by my side."

She decided to take a sip of her wine to try and disguise her trembling lips but ended up dribbling it down her chin instead. Wiping her chin with the back of her hand she looked him straight on, "You should have trusted me!"

"I know," he said quietly.

She was right, she had every right to be angry with him. He done her wrong and he treated her worse than you would an enemy, just look at today, he practically attacked her in her own home. Definitely not his finest moment in life.

"You're right, I'm sorry. I promised to protect you and always be by your side and I let you down when you needed me the most and for that I will always be sorry. I not only hurt you, but I also hurt myself, so much time I missed that I would never get." Cracking his knuckles, - Sophie knew this was something he subconsciously did when he was disappointed with himself.

Seeing him like this she couldn't help but feel sorry for him. Yes, he should have had more faith in her, in them, but she couldn't exactly blame him when her poor mother was thrown in the mix.

"As you said, what's done is done. What matters now is what happens next."

"I agree." Holding up the bottle, "More wine?" he asked, noticing she had finished hers.

"No, thank you. I'm not used to drinking any more - one glass and it goes straight to my head." She wasn't lying about that; she was starting to feel the effects already. Or maybe it was the fact they were sitting so close.

Stefano spoke, killing that train of thought, before it took shape in her head.

"What happened after? I mean, how did you end up here in London? Do you have family here?" He knew he was asking a lot of questions and he also knew he had no right to, but he had been asking himself those questions since he saw her this morning.

"No, I don't have any family here; well, my mother has a cousin here, but I don't have anything to do with them, not anymore. It's just me and Christina." Not wanting his pity, she continued, "We have Susan, she's become just like family over the years, better even," she added remembering her own family. "I met her a couple months before Christina came along and we've been friends ever since. To Christina, she's practically family."

"So, what made you move here? It couldn't possibly be the weather; it never stops raining in this place."

He didn't want to seem too intrusive or pushy, but he sincerely wanted to know how she ended up where she did.

"I always wanted to visit London and I remembered your father saying what a beautiful city it is," laughing softly, "I guess I ended up in the wrong part of town."

"How are you getting by? Do you work? I can't imagine it being easy with a kid." It just struck him that maybe she was struggling financially, that maybe that was the reason her cupboards were almost bare.

"No, it's not. Especially when you're on your own," glancing up and meeting his gaze. "But we get by. I have a part time job at a bakery which is near Christina's school. Plus, I get child benefit every month for Christina which really helps, so it's not so bad," she said, with a shrug of her shoulders.

"What's child benefit?"

"I asked Susan the same thing when she first mentioned it to me. It's money the government gives you every month to go towards your child. It was Susan who told me about it and helped me apply. It came in very handy; children grow up so fast and Christina needed clothes every other month growing up, and they're not cheap, trust me."

Stefano poured himself another glass of wine; to hell with it he thought.

That name 'Susan' was cropping up quite a lot tonight and if he was honest with himself, he wasn't liking it. She was in his daughter's life since day one and was probably with her now, he thought. Sophie spoke so highly of her and with such admiration when it should have been him, damn it!

But he was grateful that she had someone when he wasn't there for her and whose fault was that? He knew he only had himself to blame. He had always been quick tempered, and he had paid the ultimate price and so it seemed had Sophie and his daughter.

He felt ashamed, disgusted. While he spent the last few years living in luxury, his own flesh and blood was being raised on benefits from the government.

What a mess! Putting down his glass, he closed his eyes and pinched the bridge of his nose, he was beginning to get a headache.

She knew him well enough to know he was hurting right now. She wanted to reach out, to tell him everything would be ok, that it wasn't his fault, but she couldn't bring herself to say the words. Because at the end of the day, it was his fault, he left her.

Getting up and walking over to the vast windows, hoping some distance will help clear her head, she looked out, "Wow, we are really high up," she said, not being the biggest fan of heights but this view was amazing.

"It's the best view in London," he said, remembering her fear of heights.

"I wouldn't know, I haven't done much sightseeing, none actually," she found herself confessing.

"Tell me you've been to the London eye!" he asked in disbelief.

"No, never seen it. Never left north London, to tell you the truth, until today that is, to come here. I've seen it on TV though, does that count?" she added with a smile.

She felt quite silly admitting that she had moved to this country six years ago and hadn't really seen it. When she first moved here, she had been busy trying to find a place to live, then Christina came along, and things got much harder.

He stared at her reflection in the window and for the first time, he saw the depth of pain behind her eyes. He couldn't imagine how hard her life must have been the past few years.

"Well, we're going to have to do something about that then, don't we?"

His voice suddenly came out from behind her, he was standing too close, she could almost feel the heat radiating from him.

Maybe it was the wine or the brandy or both, he thought, but he found he couldn't resist. He took a step closer and placed his hands on her hips. He felt her go tense, but he didn't pull back, instead he leaned in a little closer and breathed her in.

Just the smell of her drove his senses wild. No perfume in the world could rival her natural scent.

He slowly pulled back her long silky hair from her neck and when she didn't move, he leaned down and planted a soft kiss at the back of her neck. Sophie inhaled sharply, goosebumps spreading throughout her body. He had always loved kissing that tiny beauty spot she had at the nape of her neck.

Her breathing quickened, she had to put a stop to this now before it went any further and he got the wrong idea.

Clearing her throat, she turned around and instantly knew it was the wrong move as they were now face to face, their breaths mingling.

"Stefano..."

"Yes?"

When she didn't say anything, he gently tipped her chin up, leaned forward and kissed her softly, delicately, on the lips. Then pulled back ever so slightly, enough to look into her eyes and see that she was as much aroused as he was. She still wanted him as much as he wanted her, no, scratch that, more like needed her.

He splayed his hand at the small of her back and pulled her closer, he needed to feel her in his arms, against him, below him.

He leant down and rested his head against hers, "When you're in my arms, I feel like I'm home," he sighed. The confession came out of his mouth before he could stop it, but it was true, he only ever felt complete when they were together, without her he was lost.

He placed his hand beneath her ear, when she didn't pull back, he leaned down and covered her mouth with his. It was a slow, deep kiss that made her head swirl with desire.

He savored her delicious mouth, gently pushing his tongue past her teeth to delve deeper inside the warmth of her mouth.

She instantly responded by allowing him access, moaning her pleasure against his mouth.

Somehow the contact just didn't feel enough, she wanted more. Reaching up, she tangled her arms around his neck, pulling him closer, deepening the kiss until they were both breathless.

Breaking off the kiss, he looked into her eyes and saw the same need reflected back at him. It turned him on to know that she wanted him as much as he wanted her.

Taking her hand, he started to lead her away.

She knew where he was leading her and a small part of her was screaming that she should just leave, run out of this hotel, and keep running, never to look back.

But as she looked down at her small hand in his, she realized she didn't want to walk away, she wanted this, she wanted him!

Reaching a door at the far end of the room, he looked over his shoulder and gave her a mischievous grin that made her insides roll with excitement and heat rush to her cheeks.

Stefano chuckled, "I do believe you're blushing, Miss Sophie," he said while smiling.

That had always turned him on even more. They were together a long time and had made love numerous times and in numerous positions, but she had always blushed. And he found it sexy as hell!

Opening the door, he led her inside the big room and over to the huge four poster bed.

Turning her round to face him, he ran his fingers ever so softly across her red cheek and she couldn't help but lean against his hand, almost letting out a moan. It felt surprisingly cool against her hot cheek.

He then ran those fingers through her hair and placed his hand at the back of her neck, pulling her closer to him. Leaning down he kissed her so softly that it sent shivers down her spine and made her tingle.

Instead of deepening the kiss this time, he pulled back, looking into her eyes. She knew this was his way of giving her a way out if she wanted it. A back out. She could pull back and leave, no harm done.

Instead, she placed her arms around his neck and that was all he needed, message loud and clear.

He leaned down and kissed her long and slow until she felt like she was on a merry go round and running out of air.

Letting go off her neck and bringing his hand forward, he started to slowly undo the buttons on her blouse.

Suddenly self-conscious, she pulled back, unwrapping her arms from around his neck and breaking the kiss.

She saw him grin as if he knew what she was thinking. He always did have the uncanny ability to read her mind, she thought, with a slight irritability that slowly vanished with each button being undone.

Ever since he had known her, she had always been shy. It was her character, her innocence and it was what made him fall in love with her from the tender age of fifteen.

Undoing the last button, he let her blouse slide down her arms, giving her goosebumps along the way and tossed it to the side.

Running his hand down her arm, feeling her soft skin along the way, he reached down and undid the button on her jeans.

In that moment she suddenly remembered she was wearing some very unsexy knickers, why couldn't she have worn a thong or something instead of her old granny knickers, she thought. Oh yeah, because you don't have any, she told herself. And to finish it off with the cherry on top, she didn't shave either and she wasn't just thinking about her legs!

But all too soon she found her jeans round her ankles. Holding onto Stefano's arms she stepped out of them. Now she was standing there in just her underwear and feeling that familiar warmth creeping back into her cheeks as she considered placing her hands over her underwear like a shy little virgin. And that she was not!

She should have just gone straight home. It was ok earlier out there when they were kissing, because she was fully clothed, but now she was standing here in front of this magnificent man who could only be described as a Greek god, practically naked with her granny knickers on.

He reached behind her back and in one fluid motion undid the clasp of her bra and tossed that aside too.

He couldn't help but drew in a breath at the sight of her breasts, free from their constraints. She had never been small in that department but motherhood it seemed, had tripled their size. She was a goddess to behold.

Taking his gaze back to her face he leant down and gently brushed his lips against hers, taking a step forward, forcing her to take a step back, landing on the bed. Right where he wanted her.

He leaned over her gently, pinning her beneath him and proceeded to run a trail of kisses slowly down her slender neck and to her breasts, taking his time and making her tremble.

A moan escaped her throat when she felt his tongue swirling round her nipple, gently licking and sucking while his fingers played with the other, gently tugging between his fingers.

When he lifted his head to stand up, she almost groaned in frustration, nearly grabbing his head and pulling it back down.

But immediately tensed up when she felt his hands at her knickers pulling them down, well at least they were now out of sight, she thought.

Watching him strip off his own clothes she was afraid she would start drooling, she couldn't believe the change that just a few years had done to his body.

He always had an amazing body, but this was something else entirely, the man obviously worked out! Which was a surprise as when they were together, he never did.

Letting her gaze travel leisurely from his broad shoulders down to his tight abs and lower still, she gulped at the sheer size of him. Had he always been this big, she thought with a slight tremble, or had she just forgotten what they were like, well it had been a long time.

Before she could get up and start mumbling incoherently that this was a big mistake, with the focus on the 'big,' he came back down pinning her beneath him once more.

This time taking her mouth in a long, deep kiss, his hands shaping and moulding her body, making all thoughts of leaving, a distant memory in her mind.

When she felt his hand part her legs and his fingers stroked and rubbed against her clit in the small circular movements, he knew her body craved, she shuddered with pleasure.

Smiling against her lips, he moved down to her breasts where his teeth scraped her nipple and the lap of his tongue along with his fingers working their magic, had her withering below him.

She was so hot and wet and ready for him; he couldn't hold off any longer. He wanted her, needed her so bad that he thought his balls would explode with the need.

She felt his smooth hard length press against her, and she couldn't help her reaction when she pressed her small hands against his arms and whispered, "Slowly."

Stefano registered her reaction and although confused by it, he nuzzled her neck and whispered back, "Sssh, it's ok."

With one hand on her hip, he gently and slowly pushed into her hot moist center and buried himself deep, never once breaking eye contact.

When he felt her hands on his arms slowly relax, he started to build a rhythm, nice and slow at first, relishing the feel of her around him and never wanting this moment to end.

Bringing his head back down, he covered her nipple with his mouth, first nipping with his teeth then soothing it with the lap of his tongue.

With the tempo and pleasure building in intensity, he could feel her tightening around him and knew she was close. She held on to his shoulders and feeling the smooth silky skin beneath, she couldn't help lifting her head and gently nipping him on the shoulder.

Stefano trembled and groaned deep in his throat, she always did like to bite, and it was always his undoing.

With Sophie clinging to him, nails digging deep into his back, burying his head in her neck, he plunged forward one final time and erupted deep inside her.

Sophie trembled and pulsed all around him, riding her own wave of orgasm that seemed to never end.

After spending what felt like forever lying on top of her with her arms wrapped around him trying to catch his breath, he finally rolled on to his back taking Sophie with him.

Brushing back her hair and kissing her tenderly on the top of her head while wrapped up tightly in his arms, it was easy to forget that they were ever apart.

It felt like the most natural thing in the world, it felt like home.

She let herself snuggle in closer and breathe in the scent that belonged only to him, with her arm over his waist, holding him just as tight, she drifted off to sleep.

Chapter 4

When Stefano awoke, he could see that it was still dark outside through the tiny gap in the curtains. Looking at his watch, he saw that it was only five in the morning. Whenever he was in England, he always found himself waking up at the same time, never needing a wake-up call.

He didn't adapt very easily and back home right now it was already seven, the time he usually got up.

Looking down at Sophie sleeping beside him, he instantly felt his body awakening. She truly was a beauty to behold, he thought.

How he had missed waking up to her!

As he ran his knuckles slowly down her cheek, she stirred and gave a little snort in her sleep, making him smile. He almost laughed out loud when she mumbled something about blueberries.

Thinking back to last night and the look he thought he saw in her eyes just before he entered her, was it a flicker of fear? he asked himself. He couldn't be sure, but why would she fear him or the act of love to be more precise.

It wasn't like she was a virgin; she wasn't some random woman he just picked up and didn't know. She was Sophie, the woman he once believed he would marry, and they had made love more times than he could count and not to mention the fact that she has a child!

Admittedly, that fear very quickly vanished, but it was the fact that it was there in the first place that bugged him to hell. He had spent most of last night thinking about it while watching her sleep in his arms.

One of the thoughts that had entered his head last night was that some low life had hurt her; just thinking about anyone hurting her was enough to make his blood boil.

Running a hand down his tired face, he knew they still had a lot to talk about and most importantly about that little girl Sophie claimed to be his.

He had spent far too long thinking that he had lost a child and if it turned out that she really was his daughter, then he would not lose her again.

Looking back down, he saw her slowly opening her eyes.

"Good morning, sunshine," he said smiling down at her.

"Morning," she mumbled back, suddenly realizing she was naked underneath and pulling the sheet higher up to her chin.

The move didn't go unnoticed by Stefano, who was grinning down at her.

She could feel the warmth creeping back into her cheeks as she remembered last night. Oh god, what have I done, she thought, closing her eyes, and feeling completely embarrassed.

Of all the times she day dreamed about bumping in to him and the things she would do and say, not one of them involved her jumping into bed with him.

"Water?" he offered, handing her a glass he obviously had beside him.

Taking the sheet with her, she sat up and took the glass he held out.

"Thank you." Taking a long drink, the cool water felt so good sliding down her dry throat.

So, what now? she thought to herself, while staring down at the glass in her hand. What happens now? Do they simply just part ways and try to pretend last night never happened? Or would he want to be involved in Christina's life?

Aware he was still watching her, she said the only thing that popped in her mind, "So, what now?"

"What now?" taking a deep breath, "Now we talk, agapi mou." He said, placing a finger under her chin and turning her head up to face him.

Swallowing a hard lump that had suddenly formed in her throat under his intense gaze, she foolishly replied, "What do you want to talk about?" What an idiot she thought to herself, of course she knew what they were going to talk about. She really didn't feel like the smartest cookie in the jar sometimes and who could blame her?

"I want to know everything, Sophie. How you came here, how you've been living, what happened to you, everything!" emphasizing the word.

"Where do I even begin?" She thought out loud, shaking her head.

He knew her so well that he knew if he pushed her too much, she would just close up and throw away the key.

He had always found her stubborn streak amazing but right now he really hoped it wouldn't rear its ugly head.

So, he remained silent, allowing her time to gather her thoughts.

While thinking on how to begin and what she should say, God she needed a bloody script, she thought inwardly crinching, when she noticed that he was just silently and patiently watching her. Which was a first for him as he was not a man known for his patience.

OK, here goes.

"The day we broke up was the day that nearly destroyed me," she said truthfully. Well, he said he wanted to know everything, didn't he?

"My father had kicked me out because I was pregnant or to be more precise because I was pregnant with your baby. Then you kicked me out for reasons that were unknown to me at the time."

Looking down at the glass that she was still holding on her lap, she started to run her finger along the rim, just for something to do. She hated remembering the past and what she had very nearly done.

Taking a deep breath, she continued. "I'm ashamed to admit it and may god forgive me, but I actually went to a clinic in the city looking to terminate the pregnancy."

"Now that would have made my father proud," she added.

On hearing this, he stiffened beside her, jaw tightening in the effort to not speak. He knew that if he interrupted, she might not continue and they would be back to square one, not that they had moved up a square, but it looked like they may be heading that way.

"But obviously, I couldn't go through with it," remembering that day like it was yesterday.

Because she didn't have a clue about how far along she was, the doctor had decided to perform a scan in order to date her pregnancy. That was when she discovered she was actually sixteen weeks along and when she saw the little arms and legs wriggling around, she knew deep in her soul that she couldn't go through with it.

After a while of silence he asked, "What did you do then?" as she had stopped talking and seemed far away in her mind. He knew this couldn't be easy for her but just thinking how close she came to having that abortion, tied his stomach into knots.

He would have loved to have blamed her father, but truth be told he was as much to blame, possibly more so, as he wasn't a drunk, although he was seriously considering taking up drinking as an occupation right about now.

"Then.... I left. I couldn't stay there anymore. In Cyprus, I mean."

Stefano nodded his understanding.

"As you know, it's a small village. Everyone knows everyone and everyone would have talked. You know I would have been the talk of the town, the daughter of the village alcoholic, pregnant and unmarried," she gave a snort of disgust.

"And besides I had nowhere to go, no one to turn to."

He could feel that knot in his stomach getting bigger and harder. He asked for this he thought, and the truth was always hard to hear.

"Mum told me she had a cousin over here and suggested I come. She knew just as I did that my father would never let me go back home and to be honest, I didn't want to raise my kid anywhere near that man. Anyway, I remembered you and your father saying what an amazing place London was, so I decided, why not?"

Looking up at him now, cheeks beginning to turn red, "Promise you won't laugh?"

"Laugh at what?" he asked frowning, what could he possibly laugh at.

"Strangely it made me feel closer to you. Being here, I mean, in a place where you visited."

At this confession she looked back down at the glass in her hands and started playing with the rim again, just not to look at the mocking look that must be on his face. She was such an idiot for saying that, why did she have to tell him that? She didn't have to tell him everything for crying out loud.

Well at least she didn't tell him about all those times in the first few months when she moved here, how she would constantly look at the time and think 'he must be getting up now, now he must be drinking his coffee, now he must be at work, now he must be going to bed.' She was obsessed.

But after having Christina that obsession changed. She lost count of the number of times she fantasied about bumping into him, always in some bar, all dressed up in a sexy dress, with him begging for her forgiveness and her throwing a drink in his face.

She nearly laughed out loud at how ridiculous her fantasies had been, and she had some foolish fantasies. For one, she didn't own any sexy dresses and neither did she have the body to wear one anymore. She wasn't exactly big but did go up a couple of dress sizes since having a baby, which she just couldn't seem to bloody shift. She went from a size ten to a fourteen. Not to mention her boobs were a little bigger, not that that was a problem, she thought. And secondly, she only ever stepped foot in the local pub with Susan and that was nothing like the trendy bars she saw on TV. And thirdly, which was the one that made her want to crack up laughing like a maniac, was that when she did bump into him, first she ran away from him, then she jumped into bed with him. And here we are, all in the space of a few hours!

He knew her well enough to tell by the look on her face and by the way she kept playing with that glass in her hands, not to mention the way she kept shaking her head that a lot was going on up there. If only mind reading was a real gift and didn't just belong in the sci-fi movies, what he wouldn't give to possess that ability right about now, would have come in handy six years ago too.

"What you thinking?"

"Just how things didn't turn out how I thought they would."

"What happened when you got here?"

She could feel herself beginning to tremble and it had nothing to do with being cold.

"Like I said, mum has a cousin who got married and moved here years ago when I was little. They were never close but when I turned up, she and her husband let me stay with them for a while." A new shiver ran down her body at remembering the day they found out that she was pregnant.

"Needless to say, they weren't very happy at discovering they had an unmarried pregnant woman living under their roof. So, they did what I expected them to do, they kicked me out," she said, shrugging her shoulders. "But at least they dropped me off at the local council and seeing that I was pregnant they stuck me in a hostel, where I shared a room with two other women for a few weeks. Eventually they gave me that flat where you found me, and here we are," she said.

Stefano felt numb with shock. First her father kicked her out, then he kicked her out, then to make it even worse another family member kicked her out. In another country!

He held a fist to his mouth and gritted his teeth to try and keep down the growing anger that was threatening to consume him. It all came down to him, didn't it? He was to blame for all of this. He really needed that drink right about now and seriously considering getting up and pouring himself some brandy for breakfast. Although he doubted that was strong enough for the way he was feeling, what he really needed was a shot of zivania, maybe a whole bottle. See? You, stupid fool, you have more in common with her father than you think, he thought to himself.

"How was the pregnancy? Was it easy?" he asked.

At this her voice turned colder, "No, it wasn't."

Turning her face towards the window, she only just noticed how dark it was outside, making her wonder what time it was.

Seeing her withdraw and look away, "Sophie..." reaching out and touching her on the arm.

"What?" she said, maybe a little too sharply. OK, maybe he wasn't entirely to blame but that still didn't change what happened and everything she went through alone and now here he was sitting beside her, naked may she add, and asking her if the pregnancy was easy. Well, it bloody well wasn't!

"What do you want to know, Stefano? How scared I was every single day? How I would call the midwife practically every day and do her nut in with silly questions because I didn't have anyone to explain these things to me!" she could feel tears welling up again but this time out of anger. Anger towards him, her father, her mother, and to be honest right now, at the whole god damn universe!

But she didn't let this stop her, oh no, not now. The gates were finally open.

"How when I went into labour, I was all by myself. How the pain was so excruciating, it felt like a dozen knives going through me and twisting deep inside me."

She knew she was starting to lose control now, as she was shaking so badly. She was almost too afraid to stop talking because if she did her teeth would start chattering and she really didn't want him seeing her that way. Besides, she was too worked up now to stop anyway.

"What more do you want to know, Stefano? Would you like all the gory details? I'll give you those details, shall I? Considering you should have been there! I ended up having a fourth-degree tear, how about that? Huh?"

Seeing the confused look on his face just added fuel to her fire.

"Oh, you don't know what that means? I'm sorry, I'll explain it to you, shall I? It means, I tore from one hole all the way to the bloody next because my daughter's shoulder was stuck. And because of that, I needed a blood transfusion, oh and let's not forget that while all this was going on, they discovered that I have a heart condition." She was full blown yelling now and quickly running out of breath.

"Is that enough detail for you?" she practically screamed in his face.

She was panting now.

She pulled up her legs and put her head against her knees hiding her face as she started to cry. This was the last thing she wanted to do in front of him, but she couldn't stop the tears that started to fall down her face. One thing you never did in front of this man, and that was to show weakness. She felt Stefano's hand slowly take the glass from her hand that she was still holding on to and felt him place a hand gently on her back. It seemed light and unsure which made her moan and cry all the harder.

"Sophie..." he said in a whisper.

"No, I don't want to hear it. You have no idea what I went through, how scared I was. I thought I was going to die and not see my child grow up. I was lying in that theatre room praying to god and all the saints that I wouldn't die, because I knew if I died, my baby would have no one in this world."

So now he understood why she seemed afraid last night, but wait, did that mean that she hadn't been with another man since? It sure seemed that way to him. He knew he was her first and knowing what he knew now, he would make damn sure he was her only.

He silently let her cry it all out while he kept a hand on her back, slowly caressing her smooth olive skin up and down trying to soothe her. What could he even say to make things better after everything he just heard?

Nothing he could ever say or do would ever make up for any of that, but it wasn't all his fault damn it!

Fair enough, he shouldn't have taken her father's word for it. He should have had more faith in her, in them, he'll put his hands up to that one. But she wasn't entirely blameless either, she shouldn't have up and left the country; she should have stayed, fought for them. Because if she had stayed, he would have eventually seen her growing bump and all of this, what she went through, what he went through, none of it would have happened.

She wasn't the only victim in this sorry story, he was too. He had spent too long believing she aborted his child and only he knew the nightmares that tormented his soul every night. He spent weeks, months - Christ! even years thinking and wondering where he went wrong for her to do something like that. He had thought her to be his soulmate, he had trusted her more than anyone, above all others and on that dreadful day, he believed that she had broken his trust, it was like a stab in the heart, and he had carried that blade in his ever since.

He had been with other women since, he wasn't a hermit by any means; a man has needs after all. But he had never allowed himself to get close to any of them. Getting his soul ripped apart once by a woman was more than enough for any man to handle. But truth be told there was only one woman he ever wanted more than anything and that was this amazing, strong woman sitting beside him now on the bed crying her heart out.

He noticed she had ceased crying when he suddenly heard little hiccups. It was always something that happened after she had been crying and he had always found that cute as hell.

Getting up, he put on a pair of jogging bottoms he had over a chair and walked to the other room to get her some more water from the bar, which was always stocked with mineral water at his request whenever he was in London. It was always on business, hence the strict no alcohol rule he kept, he always wanted to keep a clear head.

He could easily imagine all the staff gossiping last night when he had rung down and ordered a bottle each of red wine and brandy, to be then followed by a beautiful woman coming up to his suite. Another rule he had broken last night, but Sophie wasn't just any woman.

Sophie had felt him move from the bed and leave the room, so took this opportunity to wipe her sticky wet face with the sheet she still had over her. God, she must look a right state, she thought, most probably her face was all red and blotchy by now.

She slightly poked her head over the side of the bed, trying to see if she could locate her clothes anywhere nearby and hopefully have the chance to get dressed before he came back into the room.

Or maybe she thought, he wasn't coming back. Maybe after everything she had told him, he decided it was all a bit too much and left the room hoping she would get the message and leave without causing any drama. And everyone knew he didn't like drama! Well, he didn't need to worry his pretty little head. She'll go, it's not like she hadn't done it before.

She had found her clothes and shoes on the floor by the bed and got up wrapping the sheet round her like a towel.

Looking round the room, she saw that there were two doors, one was the door she came through last night and the other she took a wild guess to be the bathroom.

Picking up her clothes and shoes, she hurried round the bed and across the enormous sized room which she shamefully had to admit was bigger than her whole flat.

Getting to the door, relief flooded through her on discovering she had been right, and it was indeed a very large bathroom. The bathroom certainly had the wow factor, it wasn't as big as the one Stefano had back home, but it was certainly luxurious.

It had the most important item she didn't realize she needed until now, on her left. Dropping the sheet, she went straight to the toilet. She took this opportunity to have a quick look around. Opposite where she was, there was a set of twin basins with a vanity unit and huge mirror. In the far corner was a huge whirlpool bath which she would have loved to have had a long soak in, considering how she felt a little sore right now. Well, it had been a while, she thought. And on the opposite side of that, was a walk-in steam shower. Everything was pure white, silver, and gleaming.

If she hadn't already done her business, she probably would have been too afraid to sit on the loo, she thought while flashing the loo.

Putting on her bra and blouse, she noticed the only other items that she had with her was her jeans and shoes. Her knickers were nowhere in sight, they must still be in the other room, she realized in horror as she heard Stefano coming back into the room and calling her name.

"Sophie?"

Oh shit, oh shit, oh shit, she felt like kicking herself, how could she leave her knickers out there. But where were they anyway? She had picked up her clothes assuming they were in the bundle that was by the bed.

She realized she had to answer him as he was knocking on the door.

"Sophie, you in there?"

"Erm, yeah. I'll be out in a sec."

"OK, take your time."

Take your time? Was he serious?

She quickly finished dressing and combed her hair as best she could with her fingers. Looking in the mirror for the first time, she realized how terrible she actually looked, her eyes were blood shot and almost swollen shut from crying and her face was red and puffy.

Which all ended up making her feel much worse than she actually looked, if that was at all possible right now.

Get it together she told herself in the mirror. To get home, first you have to walk out there and past that man. Just plaster on a smile and walk on by, easier said than done though, she thought. She toyed with the idea of adding a 'thank you for the shag' on her way out but decided against it.

Walking to the door, she took a deep breath, opened the door, and walked out.

She found Stefano sitting at the foot of the bed, who quickly stood up when he heard her entering the room.

"I got you some more water," he said, pointing to the glass and bottle he placed on the bedside table on the side she had been sleeping on.

"I'm ok, thanks." God almighty, the man looked sexy as hell even in jogging bottoms, granted he wasn't wearing anything on top, so biceps, triceps, and all types of muscles she didn't know the names to were on display. She was beginning to feel that familiar warmth creeping back deep inside her belly.

She should go now, she thought. Because the longer she stayed here the more danger there was of her doing something stupid like jumping on that body of his and secondly, she really didn't want to suffer the added embarrassment of being asked to leave. She didn't think she could cope with that kind of rejection right now.

"Erm, I'm gonna go, I don't want to outstay my welcome." Making a move towards the door that led into the living area and her way out.

Stefano however made a move towards her, not quite blocking her way but enough to get her to stop. Well, he didn't want her to leave just yet.

They still had to talk about the future, their future, the future he thought was stolen from him, was now in his grasp.

Last night was good, great in fact; sex with somebody you cared about was always better than meaningless sex. So, no arguments there, but they didn't exactly do much talking now, did they? Yes, they talked about the past but what of the future?

"Sophie, you don't have…" but before he could finish Sophie interrupted.

"Look Stefano last night was great but we both know I shouldn't really be here and last night shouldn't have even happened. But like I said yesterday, I don't expect and neither do I want anything from you." She was fully aware she was beginning to ramble on, but she didn't care. She had to get it all out and leave for her own sanity and dignity, although she wasn't quite sure just how much dignity she actually had left.

"So, you can go back to your life, worry-free, your secret is safe with me. And it's not like I'm ever going back to Cyprus, so if you have a girlfriend over there, then don't worry, she won't know a thing."

She caught Stefano frowning at her but didn't stop to find out why, she simply walked past him, out the door, head held high, grabbed her bag from the sofa and walked out.

It wasn't until she was outside the hotel that she finally took a much-needed deep breath.

Suddenly remembering as the cold morning air hit her that she wasn't wearing her knickers. They were still in Stefano's room! Oh crap, she said out loud and stamped her foot on the ground in frustration. Luckily it was still very early in the morning and there weren't that many people around. She could only hope that he wouldn't find them, and that the housekeeper would just dispose of them.

Because she was definitely not going back up there to ask for her underwear, she would rather die a slow horrible death.

Seeing a taxi, she waved it down and jumped in.

Chapter 5

The first thing she did when she finally arrived home, was to take a much-needed shower. Pouring a generous amount of shampoo and massaging into her scalp, trying to ease the throbbing that was building up inside her head.

She felt dirty and, in more ways, than one. She felt deeply ashamed of herself, what she had allowed to happen. Just like that feeling you get when you wake up the morning after a big night out and all the memories come flooding back making you wish you had amnesia.

And let's not forget, she told herself, 'You wanted that to happen.' And having that glass of wine didn't help with her decision making either, she was such a lightweight.

After getting out of the shower, she put on her favourite and well-worn pink bathrobe. Her mother had given her this bathrobe the Christmas before she left Cyprus, their last Christmas together and every time she wore it, it was like having a piece of her mother with her.

It was her comfort.

She finally looked at herself in the mirror and quickly wished she hadn't. Her eyes were still blood shot and swollen, which wasn't surprising but at least her skin was no longer red and blotchy.

"You, silly cow," she told her reflection, suddenly feeling beyond exhausted.

She had walked back to her room and got into bed, not caring that she still had her bathrobe on or that her hair was still wet. She pulled up the duvet up to her chin, pulled up her knees and while holding on to the duvet as if her life depended on it, she started to cry.

She had predicted the night would end in tears and she had been right.

Sitting in the limo on the estate, Stefano looked out of his window and up at a window he knew to be Sophie's. A window he guessed to be her bedroom.

It was fair to say that when she had walked out of his suite this morning, he had been a little bit more than just annoyed.

When he had left the room to go get her that damn water, it seemed like he had left one Sophie just to come back and find another in her place.

However, what had infuriated him the most, was when she said she didn't need or want his help in regard to their daughter.

Not to mention when she had implied that he had a girlfriend back home whom he had just cheated on. He had been called quite a few nasty names by women in the past who had wanted the kind of commitment he wasn't willing to give them, but a cheater was never one of them. And he had been with quite a few women but never more than one at a time.

But maybe he was a cheater after all, he thought to himself.

Maybe he had cheated on all those women as he had always found himself thinking of Sophie when he had been with them. It wasn't something he would ever admit to anyone.

Somehow, it seemed like he had managed to convince himself that the reason he didn't want any kind of commitment with any of those women was because he didn't trust any woman after what Sophie had done to him. Or what he thought she done at the time. And only realizing last night that he was still in love with her; if he was being honest with himself, he had never fallen out of love with her. He had been fooling himself all these years when thinking he had hated her. But it was the plain truth, Sophie had dug herself so deep into his heart all those years ago and he couldn't get her out.

Even after what he had been led to believe she had done; he still couldn't get her out of his mind. She was that deeply ingrained in his heart and soul.

He laughed a little remembering the last woman whom he had dated for a few weeks. She had ended up slapping him round the face and telling him he had commitment phobia and would die a lonely, old man.

There was only ever one woman he wanted that kind of commitment with and ironically, she was the one running away from him!

Taking a deep breath, he closed his eyes and pinched the bridge of his nose. He was beginning to get a headache, why did everything feel so hard, damn it!

They belong together, he thought, they always had.

They have a child together and he would make damn sure his daughter was raised by both parents. He would never walk out on his kid or Sophie for that matter, nor would he ever accept visitation rights.

And he wasn't stupid either, he saw the bare cupboards with hardly any food in them yesterday. What was she feeding his daughter and herself for that matter?

It angered him to know that while he lived in that big house of his and stayed in all the best hotels, they had been living like this. In a place like this - he added as an afterthought, after looking out of the other window and spotting a group of teenage boys hanging out close by and smoking what he presumed to be weed while watching the limo and waiting to see who was inside.

No, he decided. They were going to be a family, they were going back home, one way or another. And if she didn't love him anymore, then tough shit, he thought, she would learn to love him, and he would do everything in his power to make her love him.

Waking up she looked at the time on her phone and saw that it was nearly twelve in the afternoon.

She had slept for a good three hours but still felt strangely battered and not just her body. She had ended up using muscles last night that she had forgotten she had and this morning it felt like every muscle in her body ached and burned. It felt like the day after a gym session, and she was definitely feeling the burn.

Yawning and stretching out her arms and legs all the way to her toes, she suddenly froze when she heard a knock on the door.

Is it Susan and Christina? No, it couldn't be, answering her own question. They wouldn't be knocking as they had a key.

Well, she wasn't expecting anybody today, so decided to just ignore the knocking and pretend nobody was home, she was just not in the mood today.

Curling up into a tight little ball again, she closed her eyes, hoping to go back to sleep and not wake up until the events from last night were wiped from her memory, when the sound of voices and the key in the door had her head snapping up and ears straining to hear what was being said.

It wasn't so much the key in the lock that had her heart racing, for she knew that to be Susan. It was however the very distinct male voice that had her jumping out of bed almost tripping on her duvet and landing flat on her face, while racing to the little hallway just in time to see the door slowly creaking open and she could now see Susan with Christina and Stefano following close behind.

Tightening the cords of her bathrobe, she suddenly felt very self-conscious, if she knew he was going to turn up she would have made sure she was dressed. What was he doing here? she thought.

She had thought she'd seen the back of him, especially after everything she had said to him this morning.

Her mind travelled back to Christina, because the last thing she wanted was for her daughter to get caught between them. But another thought entered her mind that instantly pushed away her fears, down into the pit where they belonged, giving way to a rising anger. Could he be here for reassurance that she wouldn't ask for child maintenance? Maybe the bastard wanted her to sign a contract, she thought. It wasn't that far-fetched, it was certainly something she could imagine him doing, that was for sure.

Well, if that was the case, then she would sign anything he wanted, as long as it got him out of their lives for good.

"Erm... wait here a second, let me see if she's home," she heard Susan saying as she opened the door and stepped in, holding Christina by the hand.

As the door opened wider, Sophie quickly ducked into the doorway of her bedroom hoping he hadn't seen her, giving Susan a quick shake of her head as she looked her way to indicate that she wasn't home. Unfortunately, she wasn't quick enough and not only she realized with utter embarrassment did he catch her ducking away, but he also caught her shaking her head.

Before Susan could even respond, and poor Susan, from the look on her face she really did look like she was caught between a rock and a hard place, Stefano stepped in behind her and said all too cheerfully, "Good morning, or should I say good afternoon?" looking down at his watch.

Looking at Susan, he extended his hand. If he was being honest with himself, he had to admit that at first, he had felt a pang of jealousy towards this woman because she got to experience everything he should have and didn't! but when he thought about how much help she had been to Sophie and how much Sophie had leaned on her, that jealousy had turned to gratitude and respect.

"You must be Susan, I heard so much about you."

To which Susan simply responded with a "Hi," and placed her hand uncertainly in his for a handshake.

Bending down to Christina's eye level and extending the same hand he said, "You must be the very famous, Christina, I definitely heard so much about you," he said with a big smile making Christina giggle and give him her little hand for a big strong handshake, shaking his hand up and down as hard as she could.

"Wow, that was a super strong handshake," he said. "Have you been working out?" making Christina giggle some more.

"No, I'm wonder woman," she said holding her head high and sticking her little chin out, in turn making him roar with laughter.

"Remind me never to get on your wrong side, wonder woman," he said with what sounded like pride in his voice.

Standing there in her bedroom doorway, her heart literally skipped a beat at the sight of father and daughter laughing together, like the most natural thing in the world.

What was he up to, she wondered? Well, whatever it was, it was going to have to wait because he couldn't just turn up here at her home whenever he wanted.

"Stefa..." before she even finished saying his name, he stood up and interrupted her.

"I was thinking I could take you both out today. You, too Susan, if you fancy it. What do you think?" going back down to Christina's eye level.

"I was thinking we can go see the London eye..." casting a quick look at Sophie then back to Christina. "Then we can go to the aquarium, what do you think wonder woman?"

Cocking her little head to one side, she asked "What's an aquarim?"

"What's an aquarium?" Christina nodded her little head. "Well, it's like a really big fish tank..." spreading his hands out to the sides as if to show how big "and it has sharks in it with really big teeth," he said, snapping his teeth.

Christina's eyes opened wide "Wow." Looking back at Sophie, she said "mummy, can we go see the sharks? Pleaseee?"

"I don't think so aripi mou, maybe next time." When he's not here, she finished inside her head.

"Pleaseee mummy, I've never seen an aquarim before." Sophie couldn't stop herself from smiling at the way she said 'aquarim' and looking at Stefano from the corner of her eye she saw him pretending to bite a nail just to stop from laughing.

"Please mummy, and we have never seen the London eye." Looking back at Stefano who was now stood up, asked, "that's the big round wheelie thing isn't it?"

Stefano chuckled and replied, "Yes, that's right. That's the big round wheelie thing and you can go up in it too." Ruffling her hair lightly.

"See, mummy?"

Sophie took a deep breath and looked over at Susan for some silent guidance, who was still standing there holding Christina's hand and looking very uncomfortable. To which Susan simply responded with a shrug of her shoulders as if to say, 'I don't know'.

She hated saying 'no' to Christina but what could she do, she only worked part time and it just wasn't always enough. So, because of that, there were quite a few no's, 'no' to the new trainers all the kids were wearing, 'no' to the new LOL toy that was out and once even a 'no' for a school trip to the natural history museum because she couldn't even afford the measly five pounds for the trip because that was the week, she had been off sick, from work and didn't get paid.

But hey, such was life, the cards she had been dealt.

Truth be told as much as she wanted to take Christina to see these places, she just couldn't afford it. Not to mention she didn't want to spend one more minute in this man's company, never mind a whole day. What was he playing at anyway, barging in here and setting her up for a fall. He must have known she would have said 'no', especially after this morning.

When another thought occurred to her, maybe he was so scared that she would bleed him dry, like a lot of women in her situation would do, that this idea of a day trip was his way of saying 'Well, I did something for you, so don't ask for anything more.'

But watching him now with Christina, she couldn't quite bring herself to believe that of him. The Stefano she used to know wasn't like that, but the years could change people, couldn't they?

She knew what her father had done, Stefano told her last night, they had talked about it, but the truth didn't stop her from feeling betrayed by him and she knew she would never be able to get the memory of him shouting and kicking her out from her mind.

One minute she was blissfully happy and the next 'bam', it was all over!

Looking at Christina's little begging face, she found herself saying, "Yeah ok, why not." Surprising herself as she planned a very stern NO, but it seemed her big mouth had other ideas.

Seeing Christina and Stefano high fiving each other and Christina jumping up and down saying "Yes", it brought such joy to her heart to see her daughter so happy about something and she had to admit, it made her feel slightly envious that it was Stefano creating this happiness and not herself.

She had asked Stefano to wait downstairs while she got dressed and got Christina ready for the day trip.

She had practically begged Susan to come along with them, but she declined saying she had some things to do. Although Sophie had the suspicion that Susan didn't want to get involved in what she probably considered family matters. After all she knew everything about Stefano and what happened all those years ago.

Before Susan had left, Sophie had shamefully asked to borrow some money which thankfully Susan kindly smiled and got her purse out, bringing fresh tears to Sophie's eyes. She had never asked this woman for even a penny but today was an exception, she didn't want Stefano thinking she couldn't provide for her own child.

She so valued their friendship and everything this woman had done for her since moving here that she didn't want money to get in the way.

She had seen firsthand, growing up, how money could destroy friendships and lives, and this was one friendship she deeply valued.

After promising to pay her back (eventually) and Susan telling her, "Don't be daft" she left, letting Sophie get ready.

She had just finished packing her small backpack which she took everywhere with her whenever going anywhere with Christina. Becoming a mother, she very quickly learned that you shouldn't leave the house without a few essentials when you have kids, when Christina poked her head through the bedroom door impatiently saying, "Come on mummy, let's go, he's waiting."

"Let him bloody wait," she said under her breath.

Taking a deep breath, she zipped up her bag and turned around facing her very excited daughter, "all ready."

"Yay," squealed Christina, rushing towards the front door, her own little mini pink backpack swaying on her back. She didn't really need a bag as Sophie carried everything they needed but she wanted to look like an adult, "just like mummy" she once said. So, Sophie got her a mini backpack for Christmas last year which she actually took everywhere with her "just like mummy," the thought making her smile.

"Hold on a minute, did you use the loo?" another important lesson she learnt after becoming a mother. Children always decided they needed the loo once you left the house.

"Yes mummy," Christina replied impatiently, "let's go."

She really didn't want to go but she couldn't stall it any longer, she had to keep reminding herself that she was doing this for Christina, that, and the fact that she didn't know how to get out of this without causing a scene and upsetting Christina.

Grabbing her keys off the hook by the door, "Let's go," she said with a big smile on her face which didn't reach her eyes.

Stefano got his driver to drop them off near the south bank of the river Thames.

As soon as Christina saw the London eye, her eyes opened wide and she started bouncing up and down in the limo. "Mummy, mummy, look at that!" she was squealing excitedly.

"I know darling, it's very big." Even though it was much more impressive seen up close rather than on the telly, she still couldn't quite let herself feel the same excitement. If it was any other time or with anyone else it would have been different.

Looking out of the window, she felt so strange sitting in a limousine watching people walking by and trying to peek inside even though the windows were tinted. There was something strange in knowing you could see other people, but they couldn't see you; granted it was better than standing in a packed London bus but strange none the less.

Even back home before the shit hit the fan, she knew Stefano's family were well off but not that well off to have a chauffeur driven limo; business must really be doing well, she thought.

Stefano reached across and undid Christina's seatbelt, setting the little girl free and just as Sophie's hand reached the buckle of hers, Stefano's tanned hand suddenly appeared over hers. "Let me," he said.

Looking up and meeting his gaze, she felt her pulse quicken and looked down as his hand slowly and gently slid from hers to the belt buckle and undid it in one fluid motion, all the while his eyes not leaving hers.

When slipping off the belt, the back of his fingers lightly grazed her nipple, making it instantly stand to attention and a warmth quickly spread down to her core making her shift in her seat. It was only a slight movement but it didn't go unnoticed by Stefano as when she looked back up, he was wearing a very cocky one-sided grin, which brought another kind of warmth to her cheeks, until that is his eyes slipped down when they caught the sudden heaving of her chest and his hand momentarily tightened on the seatbelt before letting go and moving back.

The arrogant bastard, she thought, although she found she couldn't ignore the tingling she felt when his hand had touched hers.

Stefano, it seemed, had already procured the tickets before they even got here as they were taken straight to a pod without having to queue up.

She would have to give him the money later, she thought, biting the inside of her cheek, something she always found herself doing when feeling uncomfortable. This was what she didn't want, Stefano paying for everything and her owing him money. She didn't want to owe him anything.

She was thankful however when he took Christina and lifted her on to his shoulders, then looking back extended a hand for Sophie to take, helping them both into the moving pod. The gap between the bank and pod was by no means big but for Sophie just looking down into the river below was enough to make her dizzy.

Christina was like a little bouncy ball while in the pod, going from one side to the next trying to see everything and intent on asking as many questions as possible that entered her little mind. "What's that?" she'd ask, "That's Big Ben." "Why is it called Big Ben?" before Stefano could answer she fired the next question at him "What's that?" "The houses of parliament," he answered back patiently, and this was how they went on for the whole thirty minutes they were in the pod.

Sophie just sat down on the bench that was situated in the middle of the pod, watching Christina and Stefano more rather than the London view. She had to admit, it was a spectacular view and Big Ben wasn't as big as she thought it would be, but she just couldn't tear her gaze from the two people in front of her who seemed to be having all the fun.

It was so hard watching Christina and Stefano together like this, the more she looked the more she could see the resemblance between the two and not just the facial features but their movements also. The way they stood, the way they both moved their hands when talking, it was quite disturbing to watch.

To anybody who could see them they probably looked like a happy little family out on a day trip, but she knew the truth and so did Stefano.

It made her heart ache for what could have been, all she ever wanted was for them to be a family. She would love to say it was all water under the bridge, silently laughing when thinking how fitting that statement was, considering where they were right now, but the truth was, too much had happened and she didn't find it easy to forgive and forget, not after everything she had been through.

She was deep in her depressing thoughts when Christina suddenly pulled on her arm, "Come on mummy, it's time for the picture," pulling at her to get up and stand with them for the pod picture.

Finally, when they were back on the ground, Stefano ordered a copy of the picture to be printed and when she tried to request a second copy for herself, he put up his hand and shook his head saying a second copy wasn't needed. Of course not, she thought bitterly, why would he want a reminder of today, this one was obviously meant for them.

Sophie had just pulled out her purse from her bag when Stefano beat her to it and handed over his card to the woman behind the till. She made a quick mental note of the price and put it on the list of things to pay back, no doubt that list would just get bigger as he seemed determined to keep up the act of father of the year.

It was funny really, no matter how much she struggled, she had never borrowed money from anyone before he showed up. Now she had to pay him back money with money she had borrowed, then pay that money back too. Letting out a breath, this had been the most stressed she had been in a long time.

While they were waiting for their picture to be printed, Christina was getting impatient, "When are we going to see the sharks?" she said, pulling on his sleeve.

"Just as soon as we get our picture, koukla mou."

"Oooo, how long would that take?" Christina was now looking up at him frowning.

Stefano laughed and ruffled her hair, "Not long now, I promise, and anyway the aquarium is just over there," he said, pointing behind her.

This seemed to perk her up as she looked behind her then back at him with her big eyes and a wide smile, "So we can walk it?"

"Of course, but you, my princess, shall get a ride. Your carriage awaits you, my lady," he said, as he grabbed her and put her on his shoulders.

Christina was laughing so hard that Sophie was afraid that in her excitement she might accidently pee herself but then considering she was sitting high up on Stefano's shoulders, a naughty thought entered her head, oh, I hope so, she thought, he certainly won't be able to keep up the act then with pee running down his expensive suit.

When their picture was ready which surprisingly wasn't that long considering the number of people there,

Sophie took it and they headed towards the aquarium with Christina happily sitting on Stefano's shoulders.

When they got there yet again it had seemed he had already paid, either that or they were just walking in, and nobody was saying anything.

Another so called family picture was taken and just as they were walking through the 'Enter' sign Sophie's heart nearly dropped through the glass floor she realized she was walking on.

"Mummy, mummy," Christina was bouncing on Stefano's shoulders in full on, over the top excitement. Laughing, he put her back down, pointing out a big shark swimming below her feet.

"Mummy, look at that!" Christina was practically shouting; the way children always do when over excited.

"I see, sweetie," was all Sophie could say because she had to admit this was amazing, she was completely awestruck.

She could actually see sharks swimming below her feet. She didn't even know this place existed until today.

When Stefano had left them to get ready, she had quickly done a google search and came up with the Sea Life Centre, but nothing could have prepared her for this; it was amazing.

Looking over at Christina she found the little girl lying flat on the glass floor, pressing her face against it and laughed, secretly wanting to do the same.

"Come on, this is just the beginning, there's lots more to see," Stefano said holding the little girl's hand when she got up.

Sophie suddenly found herself rooted to the spot, "Is it safe to walk on?" she asked with a nervous laugh.

She felt silly asking, as she was watching people walk past. She knew it was safe, but it was one of those questions you know you don't need to ask but you ask them anyway.

"Of course it's safe," he said with a chuckle and a big grin, taking her hand and giving her a wink.

Sophie suddenly had butterflies in her tummy, and it had nothing to do with the sharks swimming below her feet but rather with the big shark beside her who was getting up close and personal with her.

She couldn't help but like the feel of her hand in his, the way his touch had always made her feel, safe and secure, but this was a false sense of security, and she shouldn't make the mistake of forgetting that.

When they passed that section of floor, she tried to pull her hand out of his grip when she felt a slight resistance where he held on a little tighter. For a split second she thought he wouldn't let go, but it lasted merely a second and he loosened his grip and carried on walking with Christina in hand.

For a moment there she almost didn't want him to let go of her hand, she wanted him to hold on to her. She knew the feeling wasn't real, it was just a mirage, but she wanted that feeling of safety and security to go on a little longer.

What was going on with her? He was messing with her head, that's what!

She had never felt so confused and conflicted as she did now, she had to be careful and not let herself get sucked in this little game of his because it wasn't real.

Just enjoy yourself and this wonderful place because let's be honest, when will you ever be able to afford to come back here? she told herself.

And the most important thing of all was that Christina was enjoying herself. She had to keep it together long enough to just get home and then she'll never have to see him again.

They walked around the aquarium at a pretty fast pace as Christina was like a kid in a candy store. She kept running ahead but Stefano, she noticed, was always one step behind her and he made it look like a walk in the park, just like a real father would, she found herself thinking.

Despite everything she found herself relaxing and enjoying herself, there was something about being surrounded by water that she always found relaxing and growing up on an island she was always surrounded by water.

It saddened her to know that Christina would never have that same experience.

With that came the memories of her and Stefano holding hands along the beach, always in the early hours of the morning as the beach had a peaceful tranquility about it at that time of day before the blazing sun was high in the sky.

Pushing those memories back she got her phone out and started snapping some pictures of Christina who she realized was stroking a starfish. Stefano looked over at her, "Come on, have a go."

And seeing the hesitation on her face, he said, "Come on, it won't bite."

Watching Christina giggling away, she couldn't resist. Putting her phone away, she went over to where they stood and slowly put her finger to the starfish.

Wow, she thought to herself getting excited.

It didn't feel at all what she thought it would feel like, not that she'd ever given much thought to how a starfish would feel but it felt kind of prickly and soft at the same time.

"See, I told you it won't bite," Stefano whispered in her ear from right beside her. "But I might," he added.

She turned and looked at him with her finger still on the starfish, just to see him grin before being pulled away by a very eager little girl who, in her own words, was dying to see everything.

What did he mean by that? Was he flirting? Maybe he was hoping for one last shag before going back home? Well, he would be disappointed if that's what he was expecting to happen because she would never allow herself to be used by anyone, especially a man!

She decided to try and ignore him as much as possible and just focus on getting through the day.

What she really wanted to do was cut this day short and go home but that would only upset Christina who looked to be having a blast. And not to mention the number of questions a move like that would bring and Christina was not one to back down easily without getting answers. Like father, like daughter, she thought to herself with a sigh.

She closely followed them as they walked around the aquarium staying a little back giving Christina this time with her father even though she didn't know who he was.

No doubt she would ask her later tonight, shivering at the thought, as she still hadn't decided on what to say about Stefano.

She always knew this day would come but she thought she had at least a few more years to prepare. She couldn't exactly say, "Oh yeah, that's your father but I'll doubt you'll be seeing him again." He probably had a girlfriend back home or wife for all she knew.

They ended up seeing crocodiles, penguins and jellyfish among the numerous species of fish.

When they got to the gift shop which she had to admit was cleverly located near the exit, Stefano picked up Christina, placing her on his shoulders again and walked around the shop, "What do you think, should we get this giant seahorse?" To which Christina eagerly nodded her head. "And I think we should also get this penguin because it's going to need a friend, don't you think?" And again, Christina nodded, bouncing on his shoulders.

They ended up walking out with two bags full of soft toys, pencils, key rings, and a giant seahorse poking out of one of the bags. And yet again one more copy of the so-called family picture.

They had ended up eating at McDonalds. Stefano suggested an Italian restaurant to which Christina wrinkled her nose at and insisted on McDonald's, telling Stefano it was the best food in the whole world, she 'promised.'

To which Stefano reluctantly agreed and just as reluctantly ate a Big Mac and forging a "mmm, it's delicious," to a beaming Christina who had ketchup all round her mouth.

The whole day was worth this very moment, Sophie thought, hiding a grin behind her cheeseburger.

On the car ride back everyone was very quiet, each one to their own thoughts, she supposed, until she felt Christina's head on her arm. Christina had fallen asleep in her seat with her little head resting on Sophie's arm. It had been such a long day for the little girl and when the adrenaline and excitement had worn off and a big meal in her tummy, she had finally fallen asleep.

Stefano was strangely quiet. He too, spent most of the time staring out of his window. She would occasionally hear him shift position and when she would look his way, she would catch him watching her, prompting her to turn back to her own window.

She found it strange that after a whole day spent together, after playing happy family's he had absolutely nothing to say. He had spent the whole day flirting with her, with his words, his touch, the way he held her hand and she thought he wouldn't let go and now that Christina was asleep, nothing, zilch!

It just goes to show it was all a game to him, hating herself because she knew that deep down what she really wanted was for him to want her, just like the old days.

She had spent so long hating him, thinking he had done her wrong, that she didn't realize the love she had for him was still there, buried deep but still there, nonetheless.

But he did do you wrong she reminded herself, he should have had more faith in you.

Angry and frustrated tears started to well up, it was too many emotions to feel at once.

She cleared her throat and pretended she had something in her eye, the last thing she wanted was for him to notice her crying, she wouldn't give him the satisfaction.

When they finally reached the estate, Sophie tried in vain to wake up Christina, but the little girl was so exhausted Sophie found she couldn't wake her, Christina was out for the count.

Stefano insisted on carrying Christina up the stairs and for this she was secretly thankful, Christina was quite heavy for her now and to carry her up two flights of stairs she would probably get a hernia.

Once upstairs Sophie led Stefano to her room where he laid the little sleeping girl down and pulled the blanket over her.

From where she stood by the bedroom door, she saw him lean down and give Christina a kiss on the tip of her nose and in that moment Sophie's heart nearly melted, it was such a fatherly thing to do. Then he stood up and looked down at her for a few moments. Looking back at Sophie in the doorway, he headed towards her and out into the little hallway pulling the door slightly behind him so not to wake up Christina.

"Is that where she sleeps, with you?"

"Yes," was all the answer she was willing to give him. She was so tired and confused, why won't he just leave already!

Slowly nodding his head, he turned and started walking towards the front door which Sophie had deliberately kept open - hint, hint, she thought, at the time.

That was it? Just a nod of his head and now he was leaving?

Well, she should be thankful, it was after all what she wanted all day long, wasn't it?

But why bother even asking if he had nothing to say?

She was halfway taking a deep breath and thinking 'phew, he's going,' when he turned round and said, "I'm leaving tomorrow morning, I'm going back home, and I want you and Christina to come with me."

She nearly choked on her own breath if that was even possible, but knowing her luck, anything was possible.

What was he doing asking her if she wanted to go back home with him? He must obviously be expecting her to say no! if he really thought there was a chance of her saying yes, she would bet everything she had that he wouldn't have asked.

"No, we're happy here, thank you," and just to be bitchy, "and I don't think your girlfriend would appreciate you bringing a random woman and kid back, do you?"

"You've misunderstood me Sophie," his voice suddenly got deeper, "I'm not asking, I'm telling you! Get your bags ready and I'll be back here at six in the morning."

The bloody cheek on him, she thought, anger flaring up again. She had always hated this side of him, his arrogance knew no bounds.

"You're telling me?" she said raising her eyebrows, although not in complete disbelief, she did know him after all.

"If I were you, I wouldn't test me, Sophie. I suggest you get packing."

And with that he left, closing the door behind him.

She ran to her bedroom window and looked down seeing him reach the limo and before getting in he looked over his shoulder and up at her window, as if sensing she was there watching him. She quickly pulled back so not to be seen but not before catching him grin.

Chapter 6

Once back at the hotel, Stefano decided to pour himself a stiff drink before packing, not that he had much to pack anyway, he was only here for a few days.

Sitting down with his drink and kicking off his shoes, he swirled the golden liquid round in his glass, watching it as it went round, thinking how he had never come home or in this case a hotel and wanted a drink so badly. Scrap that he thought, more like needed a drink.

How quickly one can become so reliant on alcohol to make them feel better, the very thought sent shivers down his spine.

He downed his brandy in one go and slowly put his glass down on the table. What he really wanted to do was fling it across the room but had decided against it, as well as deciding not to have another one.

Damn it!

How quickly your life can change from one day to the next. Two days ago, it was just him and his half-brother and today he has a kid, a little precious girl.

He found himself thinking of his father and how during the last six months of his relationship with Sophie, before the unthinkable happened, his father had given him his mother's ring. And told him to hurry up and marry the girl because she was a 'good Cypriot girl' and he wanted loads of grandchildren.

Two years after that he passed away, not knowing that he had indeed had a grandchild in the world and never setting eyes on her.

One more thing her father had robbed his father of. It simply wasn't enough that he nearly ruined his father's business, he wanted to ruin his life and his son's life as well, and if his own daughter and grandchild suffered then so be it. The man was pure evil!

The very thought brought out a deep long sigh and nearly had him reaching for the bottle.

Life just wasn't fair, wasn't fair that his father never saw his grandchild before he died, wasn't fair that he never saw her coming into this world, never saw her first steps, never heard her first words. And it certainly wasn't fair that Sophie went through all that trauma all by herself, he should have been there by her side, holding her hand.

His heart literally sunk into a deep abyss when he realized this evening how they lived.

Christina was a very happy healthy girl and no matter how hard life was to Sophie, she had obviously put her daughter's health and well-being first. But for them to be sleeping together in the same room, the same bed, in that tiny flat just showed how much Sophie struggled and it tore his heart apart.

That's not how his daughter should be living, she should have her own room, a rocking horse, even a real-life god damn pony if she wanted one.

Well, everything was going to change now, he would see to that. He would give them everything they need, everything they could want, everything they deserve that these past few years won't even be a distant memory in Christina's mind.

She was lucky in that sense that she was young enough to forget but with Sophie it was another matter entirely.

He had already decided that he wanted his daughter in his life from the very moment he found out about her existence and had decided the same about Sophie this very morning after the night they spent together and he realized the spark was still there between them. Although spark was a bit of an understatement, it was more like an inferno, the way her body instantly lit up under his fingers, it was as if they had never been apart.

And today, the whole day spent with his little girl and there wasn't one single moment of awkwardness between them, everything had seemed so natural, and he could honestly say hand on heart that it was the best day of his life.

He had expected the girl to be shy and wary around him considering she didn't know who he was, and he was at peace with that, but instead she surprised him by being very open and very articulate.

In fact, she never stopped talking, he could have sworn that at one point she was still talking while drinking her milkshake in that awful place she loved so much.

Remembering the way Christina said aquarim, he chuckled to himself as he got up and walked to the bedroom and set about packing his bag.

He didn't need a DNA test to prove she was his, she was a Christodoulou through and through.

Reaching over to the bedside table, Sophie checked the time on her phone, it was five-thirty in the morning.

She put her arm back under the duvet and pulled it up to her chin, she would never get used to the cold here.

She was so tired but every time she closed her eyes and tried to sleep, she found she couldn't quite shut down her mind, so she had ended up lying in bed wide awake all night.

Thoughts of Stefano were swirling round her head and if he meant what he said about her and Christina going back home with him.

At first, she thought he didn't mean and secretly wanted her to say no, but the way he reacted after she said no, made her realize that he did in fact mean it.

Which got her thinking that he was crazier than she originally thought.

I mean, how on earth was he expecting this to pan out? Did he expect them all to be living under the same roof? One big happy family!

And did he have a girlfriend? He didn't mention having one but then why would he? It wasn't any of her business now, was it? But she couldn't imagine a man like him not having a woman by his side.

If he did have a girlfriend, what would she think? She obviously wouldn't be very happy with such a living arrangement, no woman would.

Or did he plan on sticking them in another house, where he would come and visit whenever he pleased, have them stashed away somewhere like his dirty little secret.

She'd seen this sort of stuff in the movies, where men led these double lives and have a whole different family living just across town from them and their other family.

And what would Christina think of all this? She would obviously have to tell her that Stefano is her father. She couldn't let her think they were just moving to another country with a complete stranger. That's if the move actually goes ahead that is!

Another thought that made her equally sick was what the people in the village would say. She had left the country a few years ago on her own then she returns with a child and still unmarried! My god, they will have a field day with that one, they were still stuck in the dark ages over there.

She did miss home, with every fiber of her being and had wished almost every single day since coming here that she could go back and not just back home but back in time.

Knowing what she now knew, she would fight for them, she would tell him it was all a lie, she would tell him she's pregnant before her drunken father turned up to spread his poison, instead of numbingly walking away like she did.

She wanted everything to be as they were back then before it all went to the shits, but with the added addition of Christina, of course; having her daughter was the best thing to ever happen to her and she wouldn't change that for the world.

Putting her arm over her sleeping daughter, she snuggled in closer, breathing her in and closed her eyes. Before she knew it, she was fast asleep.

The sound of the doorbell and a knock on the door had her jumping up in bed.

What bloody time was it? She thought feeling dizzy and extremely groggy, her mouth was so dry she couldn't even swallow and her eyes felt like she'd been swimming in sand.

The doorbell was still going as she tried to orientate herself and looked at her phone. It was ten past six.

Seeing the time, suddenly brought her back to the land of the living. That must be Stefano ringing the doorbell and knocking so persistently. If he continued like that, he was going to knock down the door.

Getting up slowly, she wrapped her bathrobe round her and walked to the front door on very unstable legs, pausing at the door.

She dreaded his reaction and what was to come, as she hadn't even started packing because a huge part of her didn't really think he would turn up, but here he was.

And let's face it, his reaction wasn't going to be a good one, considering the fierce knocking that was going on.

But then another hard knock came, making her jump and she finally plucked up the courage and opened the door, whispering, "Stop banging, you'll wake up Christina," as well as the dead, she thought to herself as she saw the thunderous look on his face and decided not to voice that last bit out loud.

Barging his way past her into the hallway, he turned round to face her, "Why didn't you answer the door?" with anger clearly taking the number one spot.

It was on the tip of her tongue to say, 'Come on in, why don't you?' but the glare she could see in his eyes told her this wasn't the time for sarcastic comments. So instead, she ended up saying something even more stupid and dangerous which she instantly regretted as soon as the words were out of her mouth. "I just did, didn't I?"

His eyes grew wide, and she could see the muscles in his jaw tightening.

"I've been knocking for ten minutes, what the hell you playing at? I thought you..." trailing off, he ran a hand over his face and walked over to the bedroom doorway and seeing Christina's little body curled up in bed, sleeping, somehow softened his approach. "I thought you left," he confessed turning back to face her.

"Left?" for someone so clever he was also incredibly stupid.

"Where would I go, Stefano? Especially in the middle of the night with a child," crossing her arms over her chest and giving him a look as if to say, go on then answer me that.

"How am I supposed to know? It can be easily done."

"Yeah, when you've got money that is," she said, stating the obvious.

He stared at her for a few seconds which felt more like minutes then he said, "You're right, I'm sorry."

She was so tempted to act like Christina sometimes did and throw her nose up in the air, look the other way and stamp her foot for good measure, but instead found herself feeling sorry for him and mumbled, "It's fine."

Did he really think she got Christina in the middle of the night and left? Was he that paranoid?

Did he really think so little of her?

"Have you packed?"

Here we go, she thought, and just like that she was back to being annoyed with him again.

When it came to Stefano, the past couple of days had played havoc with her emotions, feelings constantly changing, just like the English weather!

"No, I didn't pack," crossing her arms over her chest.

"You can't just walk into my life after all this time and tell me what to do and actually expect me to do it! I've built a life here for me and Christina, I have friends, I can't just up and leave."

"Why not? You don't exactly own this place, do you? This isn't your home, Sophie. Do you seriously prefer this place?" Spreading his hand out to indicate the small flat.

She opened her mouth to speak but before she could, "And for the record agapi mou, I didn't walk out of your life, you decided to leave the country," pointing a finger at her "Don't forget that."

"And why did I do that? Huh?" staring deep into his eyes, challenging him. "Because you kicked me out, remember?" pointing a finger back at him.

"You could have stayed."

"Stayed for what exactly?"

"You should have said something, you should have told me."

"Would you have listened? Be honest. Because it didn't feel that way to me."

Looking down and pinching the bridge of his nose, he let out a long breath.

Looking at him now, standing in front of her, he suddenly looked old, with a day's stubble on his face he looked tired, like he hadn't had much sleep last night either.

"Let's not get back into that again, shall we? What's done is done."

"I don't want to argue with you, either. But please be reasonable, we just met again literally two days ago after all this time. You have your life, I have mine, and besides, Christina doesn't even know who you are."

She could see he was about to interrupt, so she put up her hand to hold him off.

"I'm not finished yet. I done a lot of thinking last night and I thought we could tell Christina together that you're her father but let's give it some time, let her get to know you first, to get used to you. You can visit anytime you want; I won't stop you and you two can talk everyday if that's what you want. But we're not moving back to Cyprus with you, Stefano, I have made my decision," she said firmly, proud of herself. She had practiced that little speech until the early hours and had managed to get it all out without betraying the fact that she was actually shitting it.

She wasn't so much scared of him but more to do with knowing how persuasive he could be - what Stefano wants, Stefano gets.

Raising an eyebrow, "Oh, you think you have a choice?" Smirking. "There's no choice, Sophie, now pack your bags, say your goodbye to Susan and let's go home." Emphasizing the word 'home'.

"God, you always do this, you never listen."

Suddenly letting go off the anger that was slowly building up with this whole conversation, "No, you're the one not listening, Sophie. You're either deaf or too dumb to understand what I'm saying, so I will say it again and I suggest you listen carefully agapi mou: I will not be parted from my daughter after finding her, after spending years thinking she didn't make it into this world. And that little girl in there..." pointing towards the bedroom "deserves so much more than this..." spreading his hands around in disgust, "So much more than you can give her, alone. Do you disagree?"

She didn't reply, because let's face it, he was right. What could she offer her daughter? Fair enough there was the unconditional love of a mother, but children needed so much more than that, and today was the most fun Christina ever had. She wanted the world for her little girl, and she had done the best she could but sometimes your best simply wasn't enough and she knew that.

"Now pack your bags," he said, walking away into the living room, indicating the conversation was over.

Watching him sit down on the sofa with his elbows on his knees, she wanted to walk in there and argue that she wasn't going anywhere with him, but who was she kidding, seriously.

She knew he was right, what could she really offer Christina? She was on benefits for crying out loud, she worked part time at a bakery and still they struggled. Every day was a struggle, she didn't even take Christina to the supermarket with her half the time for the weekly shop, because she didn't want to have to say no to her when she would want the brand crisps rather than the much cheaper store brand or the ridiculously expensive ice-cream, as she could only afford the basics.

Life was hard here; it wasn't the land of dreams everyone thought it was. There were homeless people everywhere you looked, drug addicts at practically every corner; she couldn't even take Christina to the local park without finding syringes and used condoms in the grass.

Stefano was right, this wasn't the life for her little angel, she deserved so much more.

Feeling completely beaten, she walked to the bedroom where she sat down on the bed and watched her daughter sleep, tucking a loose strand of hair behind her little ear.

She decided to pack all their clothes first before waking her up, not that she had much to pack anyway, but more to do with not knowing what to say to her instead.

She knew Stefano, knew he was the father of her child, knew he was her one true love, but Christina didn't, she had just met the man.

How on earth was she going to tell her he was her father!

She had thought she had more time, but Stefano it seemed had other ideas.

Not that she could blame him, he always loved children, remembering him joking once that he wanted twelve children and she told him to go get a rabbit.

Remembering their time together brought a sad smile to her face, she knew deep down they will never get that back. They had their time, and the rest was brutally taken away from them, but at least Christina won't be denied her father and the life she so deserves.

By the time she had packed, Christina had woken up.

Time to face the music she thought, dreading the moment, not knowing how Christina would react.

What if she didn't want to leave England? Would Stefano accept that? Would he choose to stay here, or would he still insist on them moving, despite Christina's wishes?

So many questions were running through her head, she was beginning to get a headache, in fact since seeing Stefano again, it seemed like she had a constant headache.

She didn't need paracetamol; she needed a paracetamol drip!

Getting Christina dressed and ready, they both went into the living room together where Stefano still sat waiting for them.

The second Christina laid eyes on him, she went running and jumped into his outstretched arms. "Hey koukla mou, you're like a ray of sunshine in the mornings," tapping her nose and giving her a kiss on the forehead.

Giggling, Christina settled down beside him on the sofa looking a little shy.

Sophie decided to sit in the armchair that was opposite the sofa and not wanting to delay it any longer she decided to speak first. Well, better coming from her than him, she thought.

"Agapi mou, how would you feel if we move to Cyprus?"

"Your land?" Christina asked.

Not being able to stop a small smile spreading across her face at the way her daughter said, 'your land', she said "Yes, agapi mou, my land. How would you feel if we go live there?"

"Like forever?" Christina asked wide eyed.

"Probably, yes."

"But what about Susan? Will I see her again?"

She could see that Christina was beginning to get upset at the prospect of not seeing Susan again and so did Stefano it seemed, as he wrapped his arm around her little shoulders and pulled her closer to his side, "Of course, you will see her again. You can come and see her, and Susan can always come to Cyprus and visit. You can video call her as well every day." Tapping her on the nose.

"Is that where you can see somebody in real life on a phone?"

"Yes, in real life." Stefano answered, chuckling. She was the most adorable little girl and he wasn't just saying that because she was his daughter.

"Wow!" she said, eyes wide.

So far so good, Sophie thought, but now she felt like the contents of her stomach were creeping up as the time had come to tell her the next part.

She wanted to be the one to tell her and not Stefano, so she decided to go ahead before he got inpatient and blurted it out himself in a less than sensitive way, because Stefano wasn't a man known for his patience.

She had never faced that part of him, but plenty other people had and since they were no longer together there was nothing there to hold him back.

She didn't believe for an instant that he would deliberately hurt his own daughter but by trying to hurt her he would unwillingly hurt Christina.

"Christina mou, there's something else you need to know before we go anywhere."

The little girl just looked from Sophie to Stefano with her little hands resting on her lap, anticipation clearly on her face.

"Stefano here, well, I knew him for a long time before I came here and had you."

"I know, I recognized him from the pictures," Christina said matter of factly.

She was completely stunned and confused, frowning, "What pictures?" she asked.

"The pictures you have in the shoe box under the bed. I saw them one day when you were at work. Susan told me to put them away and I did, mummy, they're still there, I promise."

Her stomach was definitely doing somersaults now, she had never thought Christina would ever find those pictures and besides, Susan never mentioned anything to her.

She hated the fact that Stefano now knew that she still kept pictures of them and hadn't thrown them away, or even burned them like a lot of women in her position would have done.

She could feel herself getting hot, she wanted to get up and open the window, but she didn't want to give him the satisfaction of knowing she was feeling very uncomfortable.

"That's ok, honey. I believe you, you've done nothing wrong. Mummy's the one who's done something wrong." She risked a quick glance at Stefano and saw him watching her, waiting for her to continue.

"I should have told you a while ago, that the man in the pictures with mummy and the man sitting next to you now, is your daddy," she said, swallowing down the bile that came up with a vengeance. But weirdly relief spread through her that the truth was finally out. She had dreaded this day for so long, ever since she first held her daughter in her arms.

Christina looked confused, the way she always looked when asked a math question that she was trying to figure out in her head.

"But why don't you live with us? Like all the other daddies do?" she asked him.

It was a very valid question and a very mature one at that. Before she could respond, Stefano did.

"Well, your mummy and I decided it was best for you to start your education here, because it's the best in the world and we wanted the best for you..." he said, tickling her belly and making her giggle.

"And I have a business back home which prevented me from coming to get you and mummy sooner, but from now on I promise it will be more play and less work."

When she didn't say anything, "The most important thing is, I'm here now and I'm not going anywhere, ok?"

Looking up at him, she asked, "Do I get my own room?"

"Of course, you do," he said tapping her on the nose again, it was quickly becoming their thing.

"A princess needs her own room and there's a big playroom full of toys waiting for you."

Christina's eyes lit up, "And a Barbie dreamhouse?"

"Of course, there's a Barbie dreamhouse! It wouldn't be complete without a Barbie dreamhouse. And let's not forget, the beach is right on our doorstep se we can go swimming anytime we want."

"But I don't know how to swim, and I might drown," she said, looking worried.

Stefano laughed, "That's ok, I will teach you. I will never let you drown."

"Do you know how to swim?"

"Of course. Your mummy used to say that I'm like a fish in water," he said, both looking over at Sophie who responded with a nod of her head and said with a smile, "It's true."

Christina squeaked with excitement then jumped up off the sofa and said, "Can I go tell Susan that we are going to another land?"

"Of course you can, we still have some time," looking over at Sophie "Of course, if it's alright with mummy?"

Sophie knew how much Christina loved Susan, she did too and would never deny her this, "Of course, you can my love, I'll be down myself in a minute."

When Christina was out the door Sophie looked over at Stefano and mumbled a "Thank you." She hadn't expected it to go the way it did, and she hadn't expected the explanation that he'd given Christina about why he wasn't around. It completely threw her!

She had expected him to be a bastard about it and who could blame her, considering his recent behavior.

"For what?" frowning.

"For what you said to Christina, about her education and work. Thank you for not putting the blame on me."

"I think we've both been hurt enough, there's no sense in hurting her as well. And besides, I think we're both to blame, don't you?"

Looking up into his eyes, for a moment she thought he was going to say something more but then he shook his head, as if he was shaking the thought away and got up.

"You should finish packing and go see Susan; I'll be downstairs in the car. We have about thirty minutes before we have to leave," he said, looking at his watch.

"By the way, this Barbie dreamhouse, is it a real thing?"

"Yes, it is, google it," she said with a laugh.

Well, let him work for it, she thought, as he turned to leave.

When he reached the door, he looked over his shoulder at her and said in a quiet voice, "I don't blame you, by the way."

Chapter 7

Stefano had stuck to his word and gone back to the car and since she had already packed, she decided there was nothing left to do so she locked up and went downstairs to join Christina in saying goodbye to Susan.

She would miss her friend dearly and felt an ache in her chest at the thought of not seeing her daily.

Over the years they had become so close that she saw Susan as family. People like Susan and the friendship that had naturally developed between the three of them made sayings such as 'blood is thicker than water' so ridiculously false.

Where her family had been ashamed of her, lied about her, abandoned her, Susan had done none of those things, she was always by her side, helping and supporting her through thick and thin.

She honestly, hand on heart, didn't know how she would have got through the past few years if it wasn't for Susan.

She hated leaving like this, so suddenly; she owed her so much more than just a quick goodbye, but Stefano didn't give her much choice.

Stepping into Susan's flat she could instantly hear Christina's excited voice telling her all about the playroom and all the toys she would probably have. That girl had a wild imagination, she thought, shaking her head.

"...there's going to be a Barbie dreamhouse with a slide, an LOL camper van with all the LOL dolls. Of course, a rocking horse and probably a ball pit," clapping her hands together excitedly. Susan was simply nodding her head, smiling, and trying to look just as excited as Christina.

"Hmmm and probably a swing and slide as well," she added in, while tapping a finger against her chin.

"I don't think the playroom is that big!" Sophie said walking into the living room.

"Mummy, mummy," running up to her and jumping into her arms.

"I was telling Susan all about my new playroom and daddy."

"I know, I heard," putting Christina back down. She was getting way too heavy for her now.

"Have you said your goodbye to aunty Susan? Or did you just chew her ear off about the playroom?"

"Yes mummy," she said, smiling up at her.

"Mmm, yes to which one?" she asked.

"Both," she responded with a giggle.

"You cheeky little thing," laughing down at her daughter's happy face. This was the happiest she had ever seen her.

"Go on, go downstairs, Stefano's waiting in the car." Giving her a quick kiss on the top of her head, "I'll be down in a minute."

"Ok mummy." Running into Susan's arms, she gives her a big hug and kiss, "I love you, aunty Susan." Then ran out the door.

Sophie looked back at Susan and let out a sigh.

"Is it true?" Susan asked.

"Yes, it's true."

Susan patted the sofa beside her, "Come, sit down. Tell me what happened, but first, are you ok?"

"Not really, but I will be. I hope."

Sitting down next to her friend, she told her everything that happened, all that was done and said the last couple of days.

"And we just told her, after he insisted last night that we move back to Cyprus with him. To tell you the truth, Susan, I didn't think he actually meant it. But then he turned up an hour ago and demanded that I pack, what could I do?" putting her face in her hands, tears threatening to spill.

"I don't want... I can't lose Christina." Trying to hold in the tears.

Feeling Susan's hand on her back, she looked up and into her friend's gentle face.

"It will be ok," she said gently.

"I have to tell you, Sophie, I think it's for the best. This is no place for a little girl to be raised and you've never really been happy here, let's be honest, who is, in a shithole like this?" she said, looking around her.

"You're lucky he wants to take responsibility and support you both, you know how many women want that and don't have it? You were one of those women until now. It will work out, you'll see. And try to remember that he is a victim in this, too, your father may have lied about you, but he lied to him too! He wanted to hurt him and at the same time he underestimated you."

"I know, but it hurts to be around him." The tears were beginning to fall.

"I know, honey, sssh, don't cry, don't let Christina see you cry," she said, rubbing her back.

"Will you visit?"

"Hell, yeah," she said, making Sophie laugh. "I'm gonna hit that beach and come back looking like a lobster. And to see you, obviously," she added with a cheeky grin making Sophie laugh even harder.

She always had a way with turning her tears into laughter, what would she do without her now?

Giving her a big hug, "You can come anytime and I'm going to call you every day."

"Ok, well let's not take it that far." Again, making Sophie laugh, but this time when she pulled back, she saw that the other woman had tears in her eyes, too.

"Look what you've done to me now," she said to Sophie, stifling and wiping away a tear.

"Seeee, you loveee me," Sophie taunted.

"Of course I do, you silly mare," Susan said slapping her on the arm and Sophie pretending it hurt. "Ouch!"

"Seriously, you'll be fine, you're stronger than you think. And you know I'm always here for you, don't you?"

"Yeah, I know."

"You can call me anytime, day or night. And if it doesn't work out or you're unhappy for any reason, just call me and I'll bring you right back, ok?"

"Thank you," she said as the tears were sliding freely down her cheeks.

"Oh, come here, you," Susan said, pulling her into her arms and kissing her on the side of her head.

"I'm really gonna miss you."

"Ohh, I'm gonna miss you too, hon, but remember we will see each other again and I'm just a phone call away."

Just before leaving Sophie tried giving back the money she had borrowed the previous day, but Susan would have none of it, instead she ended up giving her an extra couple of hundred and wouldn't take no for an answer.

They had decided that Susan wasn't going to inform the local council straight away of Sophie's departure. She would wait a couple of months for Sophie to see how life in Cyprus was going and if all was well, then she would inform them and if not, then at least Sophie still had her flat to come back to. The last thing she needed was to find herself homeless!

Walking down to the car, she turned around and took one last look at her bedroom window on the top floor, then her eyes travelled down to Susan's window where she found her friend looking out, waving with one hand while dabbing at her eyes with her other.

Waving back, she then turned round and got in the waiting car where she found Christina and Stefano playing a game of rock, paper, scissors.

The flight back was just as bad as the flight out of here had been. Granted she was now flying first class with more leg room, champagne, and an actual menu but it couldn't take away from the fact that she still hated flying and heights in equal measure.

Christina on the other hand, fortunately, didn't seem to suffer from the same phobias she had. She did however suffer from travel sickness and Sophie had completely forgotten to buy some anti-sickness medication from the airport.What did surprise her, however, was how well Stefano handled the situation when Christina puked all over herself. Taking charge and holding Christina's hair back, even taking her to the tiny toilet on the plane and getting her all cleaned up. When she had tried taking over, he had insisted it was his pleasure. So, she did the only thing she could, and that was to sit back and try to relax, let him see how hard parenting could be. He'll soon come back, all grossed, out asking for help, she told herself, smiling.

But instead, Stefano and Christina, who was now wearing a new clean top, both walked back to their seats looking happy and laughing together.

"What's so funny?" she asked.

"Nothing." They both replied at the same time, giggling.

Were they laughing at her? she thought. She was beginning to get paranoid, that's your daughter for crying out loud, with her father, just having a giggle, nothing to get paranoid about. But she couldn't help feeling left out and she didn't like the feeling.

The rest of the journey had gone smoothly and now they were sitting in the back of a limo going past groves of olive trees. Everything was so dry and hot here, she had forgotten how hot it got here in the summer. Stepping out of the plane had been like opening the oven door and getting hit in the face by the hot air.

Christina had finally fallen asleep. Surprisingly she had spent the entire flight here wide awake but the minute she entered the car she had fallen into a deep sleep and instead of resting on Sophie, her little head was resting on Stefano's lap where he absent mindedly caressed her head while looking out the window in silence.

She had been away for a very long time and didn't remember the way; not that she was any good with directions anyway, she could get lost in the local supermarket. But she was sure this wasn't the way to Limassol.

"Stefano, where are we going? This isn't the way to Limassol, is it?"

Turning to face her, "No, it isn't. We're not going to Limassol; I live here in larnaca now."

That was all he said, he didn't mention that the reason he moved here in the first place was because he couldn't bear living in the old house because every room, every corner had reminded him of her and everything he had lost.

"Oh, ok," was all she could say, she didn't know how she felt about that. She wished he had the decency to have told her before they got here. She didn't handle change very well and he knew that about her.

She should be pleased in a way, at least she wouldn't have to deal with all the gossip, whispers and stares that was all too common in a small village. At least here nobody knew her.

Suddenly she could see the beautiful blue water of the ocean, sparkling like a million diamonds in the distance. Winding down the window, she took in a deep breath. She could smell the saltiness in the air already.

"It has a certain calming effect, doesn't it?" It was more of a statement rather than a question, she realized when she took a glance and saw him looking in the same direction.

"Did you miss it?" he asked, this time turning his attention towards her, he couldn't ever imagine living anywhere else.

"I missed a lot of things," she answered truthfully, but not giving him the satisfaction of telling him exactly what she missed or who to be more exact.

She resumed looking back out the window and very soon they were pulling up in front of an amazing villa. He sure wasn't exaggerating when he said the beach was right on his doorstep.

"Home sweet home, agapi mou," he said, and looking back at him she couldn't quite keep down the feeling of disappointment that sprang up when she realized he had been talking to their daughter.

Scooping the sleeping girl in his arms, he got out of the car and bending down, "You coming?" when she still hadn't moved.

Of course, she was coming, where else would she go? It's not like he gave her much choice now, was it?

Taking a deep breath to steady her nerves at what came next, she got out and walked behind him to the front door which was suddenly opened by a woman whom Sophie instantly recognized as Eleni, the housekeeper Stefano's father had back in Limassol.

So much for no one knowing me, she thought.

"Stefano," she said, clasping a hand to her chest, "She's the spitting image of you, my son."

So obviously he had been in touch and told her about Christina before they had even left England.

"You really think so?" he asked looking down at her in his arms, voice full of pride, shocking Sophie.

"Of course! I just hope on the personality front, she takes after her mother," she said, looking past him and winking at Sophie.

Coming towards her and pulling her into a big hug, "Come here, my dear, we've missed you."

"Some more than others," she added with a whisper before letting go and pulling back with a big smile.

What did she mean by that?

Well, this was certainly not the welcome she had expected. In fact, she hadn't expected any welcome.

"Come, come, you must all be so tired after the long flight" ushering them inside and closing the door behind them.

"Stefano, take the little girl upstairs to her room."

"Is it all ready?"

"Of course," she answered enthusiastically. "Now go, and I'll show Sophie to her room."

Stefano walked up the stairs first, taking each step slow and steady so not to wake up Christina who seemed perfectly comfortable in his arms.

Eleni and Sophie followed close behind and when realizing Christina's room was next door to hers, she breathed a sigh of relief.

They had spent so long sharing the same room, the same bed, that it was going to feel strange not being together tonight, but at least she could sleep with the knowledge that she was just in the room next door.

"Don't worry about your bags, dear, Stefano will bring them up soon."

She was about to protest to that and say she could get them herself when Eleni left, closing the door behind her.

Looking around the big room, which was just as big as the hotel room, she noticed the huge glass doors which led on to a balcony on her left and went straight to them looking out and seeing the beautiful blue water.

What a sight to wake up to every morning!

Opening the double doors, she stepped outside on to the balcony, breathing in the fresh salty air when she heard the bedroom door opening. Stepping back inside the room she saw it was Stefano with her bags.

Putting them down by the door, he straightened up, "Beautiful view, isn't it?"

"Yeah, it is." Crossing her arms over her chest, thinking how awkward this felt, one day they were arguing and the next she was in his house, and he was talking to her about the view!

"Is Christina still asleep?" she asked. She hated being separated from her.

"Sleeping like an angel," he said, watching her cross her arms.

He tried not to make it obvious but couldn't help but notice how her breasts pushed up and out when she crossed her arms.

Feeling himself going hard and wanting nothing more than to pin her down beneath him, it didn't help knowing that now was not the time, he needed to gain her trust again and that was definitely not the way to get that.

Not knowing what else to say to him, she started to look around the room; this was beginning to get uncomfortable again. Instead of leaving after bringing her bags, he was still here ogling her breasts. Did he really think she didn't notice? Well, her body certainly did as she realized her nipples were suddenly straining against her bra.

"Eleni made moussaka, if you're hungry."

At the mention of food, as if on cue, her stomach started to growl.

Shit! Did he hear that?

"I'm fine for now, thank you."

Her mouth was starting to water, moussaka was her favorite and Eleni's was the best in the world. But somehow and for reasons she couldn't quite understand, she found herself turning down the meal, even though she was absolutely starving.

Maybe she could sneak down to the kitchen later and have some, she thought.

My god! Was she going to be eating in secret from now on? This was insane.

In her defense, all this happened so quickly, she just needed time to think, to adjust. Stefano bombarded her with so much in such a short space of time that she couldn't think straight.

Yeah, that was it. She wasn't going crazy, not yet anyway.

If only he would just leave and let her get some rest, she was knackered.

Walking over to the huge bed, she sat down faking a yawn. Well, it started off as fake but then turned into a real one halfway through.

"God, I'm really tired, think I'm going to get an early night, it's been a long day." Hint, hint, she thought.

When she saw him turning round, for a split second she thought he was going to leave. But that train of thought however had been quickly dashed when instead of walking out the door, he instead closed it and proceeded to walk towards the big oak wardrobe at the far end of the room.

"What are you doing?" she asked frowning.

"Don't worry, I got the hint. I'm just going to get changed first." He said, as he opened the wardrobe and took out a pair of denim shorts and a t-shirt.

Watching him walk over to a cream colored cuddler chair situated in one corner by the balcony doors, she quickly looked the other way when he started to undress.

Stefano noticed the blush that he had always found so sexy had crept into her cheeks, even though she tried to hide it by looking the other way, but not quick enough, which made him instantly regret the constricting shorts he chose to wear.

He had to get out of this room before he did something he would later come to regret.

"Why are you getting changed here?" she asked rather too abruptly.

"Why?" not liking her tone one bit.

Turning round to face her as he was pulling down his t-shirt, "Because, this is my room." He stated, coming to stand at the foot of the bed, towering over her and forcing her to look up at him.

"I thought..." biting the inside of her cheek, she wasn't quite sure what to say to that.

"Yes?" raising an eyebrow, of all the years he'd known her, he never seen her speechless and if he was honest, he secretly liked it - this reaction she was suddenly having around him.

Of course, he didn't need her saying it, he knew what she had been thinking: she thought she had this room all to herself. Big mistake, he thought to himself. If they were doing this, they were doing it right, with her in his bed, ideally below him.

"I just thought that you would be in another room." Looking up at him, she thought she saw a small twitch of his lips.

"Well, you thought wrong."

"Well, I'll sleep with Christina then." That defiant glint in her eyes obvious.

"Christina was promised her own room and as you know, I never break my promises."

"So where do I sleep then?"

This time all defiance was gone and in its place was a vulnerability he had never seen in her before. He wanted to reach out and comfort her but knew she would only push him away. No, he had to be firm.

"Well, you have two choices, my bed or a hotel. You decide, but I know what I prefer." Giving her a wink and turning round, he walked out, closing the door behind him.

As soon as the door was closed behind him, she buried her face in a pillow and allowed the tears to fall freely, not that she could stop them.

She simply curled up into a tight little ball and allowed them to completely take over.

"Shall I take a plate upstairs to her?" Eleni asked.

"She will come down when she's hungry," Stefano responded, taking another mouthful of aubergine.

Tutting and shaking her head at him, "Stefano! She's not a cat." Scolding him.

"She's also not a child, but she's still behaving like one."

"You think you are behaving any better? You are just as bad."

"I'm not the one hiding away, at least I'm trying."

"Are you? Or are you just dictating to her? Just remember, she isn't one of your employees, Stefano, she's the mother of your child. It's Sophie," the older woman added in before going back to her food.

Sitting outside on the terrace enjoying his meal with Eleni and her husband, Costa, he did think about taking a plate of food upstairs for her before Eleni even mentioned anything and leaving it outside the room for her. He knew it was her favorite meal and so did Eleni, which is probably why she made it.

Sophie and Eleni had always got on like a house on fire and the older woman was over the moon when he called, telling her all about Christina and how they were both coming back home with him. And she didn't have the decency to come down and eat the meal he knew took Eleni all day to prepare, so in the end he had decided against taking a plate upstairs for her.

If she was going to behave like a child, then he would treat her like one.

He had already done more than enough to proof to her that he was here for them both, that he wanted to be in their lives, that he was a loyal and committed father, and very soon, husband!

Because one thing was for sure, he would not allow anyone to call or even think of his daughter as a bastard.

That was the original plan anyway back then before the shit hit the fan. Get married, have children, and live happily ever after. So, they had the child first, so what? He thought to himself. If he knew she had been pregnant back then, if he didn't believe her father and if she didn't run, he would have had that ring on her finger a long time ago. But what's that saying? Better late than never!

He knew without a shadow of a doubt that she still had feelings for him, the way she blushed around him, the way her body responded to his that night, it was just like old times. He could just feel it in his bones.

The question was, was she so consumed with anger that she couldn't see what was below it?

She was hurting, her life had been an uphill struggle the past few years and he understood that, he more than understood that! He'd been living in the same hellhole, being tormented every single night by those god damn nightmares!

He would give her space, for now!

Waking up the next morning, the light filtering in through the balcony doors, she was momentarily confused about where she was.

Hearing the sound of running water quickly brought her to the here and now, realizing that it must be Stefano in the en-suite having a shower.

She felt him getting into bed late last night, had felt him lean over and stroke her cheek with a finger and even though her heart skipped a beat at his gentle touch, she kept her eyes closed pretending to be asleep.

Here they were, together with Christina in this beautiful house, sharing a room, a bed - it was everything she had ever wanted but somehow it felt tainted by the past few years and by everything she had believed to be true at the time.

Checking her phone and seeing it was only six in the morning, she toyed with the idea of going for a walk along the beach. It had always been her favourite time of day and considering that Christina wouldn't be up for at least a couple more hours, she decided it was a good idea to clear her head in the fresh morning air before the day turned into a furnace again.

Just as she got dressed, she heard Stefano's phone ping with a text and shamefully curiosity took over.

She didn't know why she did it, well she did, she was jealous, plain and simple. The idea of him with another woman tied her stomach into knots, even though he had every right.

It wasn't like they were a couple, was it? So, he could do and literally DO anyone he wants.

Still, she reached out and took his phone where she found quite a few messages from a woman called Vicky.

'MORNING AGAMI MOU.'

'CAN WE TALK?'

These were sent just now but there were a few messages from last night on there, looking over towards the bathroom door and satisfied she could still hear the shower going, she scrolled down reading on.

'ARE YOU BACK HOME?'

'CAN I COME ROUND?'

'I'VE BEEN THINKING ABOUT WHAT YOU SAID, CAN WE TALK?'

'I LOVE YOU, BABE.'

So, she had been right, he did have a girlfriend and the bastard cheated on her with her!

He really had changed, he wasn't the man she used to know, the man she used to know wouldn't do something so vile. Putting down the phone she left the room.

Poking her head through Christina's door and assuring herself she was still fast asleep, she closed the door and made her way outside to the beach.

Stepping into the room after having the longest cold shower on record, well he certainly needed it after spending the night with Sophie in his bed and not being able to touch her.

Watching her breasts rise and fall with each breath she took, he could have sworn his balls had turned a shade of blue by the morning.

He immediately noticed upon entering the room that Sophie wasn't in bed or even in the room. Checking his phone for the time, he saw that he had received yet another message from Vicky. That woman just didn't take no for an answer. What exactly they needed to talk about he had no idea. They had only dated for a few weeks, and he had already broken up with her before going to London.

Putting the phone back down, he decided it was best to just ignore her, she would get the message soon enough.

Putting on his clothes he walked over to the double doors and looked out at his favourite view which was only topped by seeing Sophie walking along the beach.

Instantly he was reminded of all those mornings when they would wake up early, get in the car and drive to the beach just to enjoy the sand and water between their toes and watch the sunrise.

Often, they spoke of their future together, everything they wanted to do but sometimes they just walked hand in hand in silence, words not needing to be used. That was the thing with Sophie - they could always sit in silence and still be completely comfortable. He hadn't found that with anybody else since.

Time to step up and reclaim what's his, ideally before his balls drop off.

She couldn't explain it but since seeing those messages on his phone she couldn't help but feel betrayed, almost like she had been cheated on.

She knew she was being unreasonable, but she couldn't help how she felt; what confused her the most was why she felt that way. Was it possible that she still had feelings for him?

She just needed some space and time to figure all this out.

"Morning," came the sound of Stefano's voice behind her, making her jump.

She had been sitting down enjoying the feel of the water coming up to her feet when he came and sat down beside her.

Raising her eyebrows in acknowledgement, she continued to look straight ahead. She refused to let him ruin this moment for her. She hadn't felt the sea and sand on her feet in so long, she was going to damn well enjoy the moment.

"I checked in on the little princess, she's still fast asleep."

"So did I. Christina won't be up for another hour at least. English time, remember?"

She heard him draw in a breath at that last comment.

"That's fine, Eleni can get her dressed and ready if you want to get some rest and enjoy the sunshine. I guess you didn't get much of either back in London."

What's he trying to do, push her out? You rest, I'll get her ready, I'll get her fed, I'll get her to school, to the doctors and before she knew it, she was out of Christina's life.

Well, that wasn't going to happen. Over my dead body, she thought.

"I can get my own daughter ready, thank you."

Frowning, "I know you can, I just thought..." before he could continue, she cut him off.

"Well don't," she wasn't willing to have this conversation with him now or any conversation for that matter.

"I have to go, I have a meeting, but I'll be back early," he said, getting up.

He still had some time to kill but could see she wasn't in a talking mood, so decided to let her be for now.

"Take your bloody time," she whispered under her breath.

"What was that?"

"I said, have a good time."

He knew she was lying as he had heard every single word she had said. "Thank you, same back to you."

As he began to walk away, he just about caught her saying 'bastard', which brought a smile to his face and annoyingly made his cock go hard. His feisty Sophie was still in there and he was planning on drawing her out.

Walking back to the house, she soon found the kitchen on the ground floor and found herself impressed with the sheer size of it, falling in love with it instantly.

This was her dream kitchen. She could easily imagine herself cooking and baking in here all day long and just as quickly had to remind herself that this wasn't hers. It didn't mean she couldn't appreciate the beauty of it though.

Seeing Christina sitting at the island in the middle of the big room with Eleni, she walked right over and gave her little girl a big hug and kiss on the top of her head. It truly did feel strange seeing her now after spending the night apart. She missed her, like the air you breathe suddenly being taken away from you.

"Oooo that looks nice," she said, peering over her shoulder and looking at what she was eating.

"It's Greek yogurt with honey and nuts. It's Greek, mummy, like us," Christina answered with yogurt still in her mouth.

"Really? Well, you certainly seem to be enjoying it," laughing, as Christina was enthusiastically nodding her head.

"Good morning, Sophia mou, would you like some?" Eleni asked, getting up.

"Actually Eleni, can I be really cheeky and ask if there's any leftover moussaka? It's ok if there isn't," she added quickly, not wanting to offend.

With a big wide smile, "Of course there is, my dear, I saved you a big piece."

Getting it out of the fridge and heating it up for her in a microwave that almost resembled a full-sized oven, she placed the plate in front of her in no time, at which point Sophie was nearly salivating.

Leaning in and giving her shoulder a squeeze, "You know, I made it for you, not for him," she said giving her a warm smile and instantly making Sophie comfortable.

Bless her heart, she remembered this was her favourite meal.

"I'll get you some Greek coffee."

"Oh, no coffee, thank you."

"What? No coffee? But that's a sin!" Eleni joked, doing the sign of the cross.

"You're not following one of those health crazes they have over there in England, are you?" "Well, you do know too much coffee is actually bad for you."

"Yes, yes." Then added, "How about juice?"

"Yes please, thank you," she said, laughing.

Pouring her a glass of freshly squeezed orange juice and placing it in front of her while Sophie was busy shoving mouthfuls of moussaka into her mouth. She might have been starving since yesterday, but this really was the best moussaka in the world.

"Thank you, this is just how I remember it," she said between mouthfuls, making the other woman laugh.

"I'm glad you're enjoying it my dear," she said and went about her duties but not before she gave her a tender kiss on the head and said, "Welcome home."

Which instantly brought fresh tears to her eyes. She had always been fond of Eleni and her husband, and it was nice to see that Stefano had brought them with him and didn't leave them when he moved here.

"Mummy, you have to see my playroom, it actually has the Barbie dreamhouse I always wanted!" excitement clear in her eyes.

"Does it?"

"And lots of other toys too." Bouncing up and down on her seat.

"Oh wow, well, once we finish eating you can show me." When faced with her daughter's excited face she couldn't help feeling her excitement. When Christina was happy, she was happy.

That's how it should be, how all parents should be, unfortunately her father must have been absent during that lesson.

When Christina finished her breakfast, she sat there on her stool huffing and puffing, and tapping her fingers on her empty glass until Sophie put her last forkful into her mouth, well, she wasn't going to waste good moussaka.

Before she could even swallow it down, Christina jumped down from her stool grabbing her by the arm, started to pull in the direction of her bedroom.

Once in Christina's room, Sophie was led through a door on the right which led to her very own playroom.

And man, was it a playroom!

It was almost as if Christina's wild imagination had come to life. There was, of course, the much talked about Barbie dreamhouse, a huge merry go round style rocking horse, what looked like the whole LOL collection, mini trampoline, amongst a load of other toys.

She couldn't believe her eyes, one word that popped into her mind was WOW and HOW - ok that was two words, but how in the world did he manage all this in less than twenty-four hours.

It looked like an actual toy store!

"Mummy mummy, look I have a twapoline." Jumping up and down on a very impressive trampoline, making Sophie burst out laughing at the way she said trampoline. When she got too excited, she would talk too fast which in turn caused her to make simple mistakes, but they were cute mistakes.

Putting a hand to her mouth, she looked around the room not quite believing what she was seeing.

He really did all this?

If she hadn't felt conflicted before, then she certainly was now.

"And look mummy, I have a tent." Jumping off and leading Sophie to the tent.

Crawling inside she saw it was actually filled with books on the one side and on the other were throws and pillows scattered on the floor with fairy lights above, creating a cozy little reading nook.

To say she was impressed was an understatement.

Christina picked a book for Sophie to read. Of course, halfway through she jumped back up and out, pulling Sophie with her.

They spent the whole morning playing together in her new playroom. By the time Stefano came back home he found them busy at play with the tea party set which was complete with a little round table, three little chairs and a red and white check tablecloth to complete the look.

She didn't know how long he had been standing there for, but when Christina shouted out 'daddy daddy' and jumped out of her seat, Sophie nearly fell off hers.

He had obviously come straight up from work as he was still dressed in his trousers and shirt, just the tie was missing and a couple of buttons were undone on the collar, giving him a rugged look.

"There's my girl," he said, wrapping his arms around Christina who flung herself at him.

"I see you found your playroom," giving her a kiss on the nose.

"It's the best in the whole world," wrapping her little arms tightly around his neck.

Walking over to the tiny table with Christina tightly wrapped around him, he sat down at the little chair with Christina turning round and settling on his lap, giving Sophie a nod. She smiled back.

"Daddy, we've having a tea party, would you like to come to my party?" she asked, looking up at him.

"Oh, that would be nice, am I invited then?"

"Of course, you are silly."

"Silly? Silly?" tickling her on the tummy and arms, making her squirm and giggle.

Handing him a tiny teacup while picking up her own, she clicked her cup to his, saying 'cheers,' then doing the same with Sophie.

"Cheers, mummy."

"Yeah, cheers, mummy," Stefano, giving her a wink over his tiny teacup and pretending to drink from it.

After the tea party was over, she found herself sitting back on the little chair in the corner watching Christina and Stefano playing together.

At the moment Stefano was the 'horsie' and Christina was on his back, she had pointed out earlier that there was huge rocking horse literally beside her but Stefano replied that it was more fun this way. Bet he won't be saying that by the time Christina was done playing this game.

She had to admit, watching them playing together like this, made her heart and soul, both flutter.

They spent most of the afternoon like this, playing together, with Stefano involving Sophie in the play as well and enjoying a plate of sandwiches which Eleni had brought up for them.

When they were like this it was easy to forget they were no longer a couple.

They were all having so much fun, they didn't realize what time it was until Stefano's phone rang and they realized it was nearly dinner time.

Getting up off the floor, he fished his phone out of his pocket and with a frown creasing his forehead, dismissed the call.

Looking back at Christina he said, "How would you like a picnic on the beach?"

"Yay, a picnic." Jumping and down.

"Ok, you stay here with mummy, and I'll go get things ready and I'll come get you both, ok?"

Nodding her head and wrapping her arms around his torso giving him a bear hug, then running off and jumping on the trampoline.

Turning to Sophie, "She seems happy, doesn't she?" as if seeking reassurance.

For the first time since knowing him she could see doubt in his eyes. She felt bad for him, for she knew the feeling all too well.

"She is, the happiest I've seen her, actually. Thank you," she added.

"How did you do all this so quickly?" she asked, spreading her arm around to indicate what she could only describe as a toy store.

Chuckling, "I made a lot of phone calls," he admitted.

"Thank you," she said looking up at him. This was every girl's dream, and he had made it happen.

"No need to thank me, it's my duty to keep you both safe and happy."

Raising a hand, he brushed the back of his fingers along her cheek and when she didn't flinch or move back, it gave him hope that maybe all was not lost after all.

"I won't be long." Blowing a quick kiss to Christina which she pretended to catch, he turned and left the room.

Sophie couldn't help but laugh out loud watching Christina having the time of her life. She had resembled a little bouncy ball ever since Stefano entered their lives.

If she was being truthful, she actually enjoyed herself today, too.

Stefano always had this aura about him, had always been able to make her laugh and forget her worries, even it seemed, when those worries were about him!

She could still feel the touch of his fingers on her cheek from when he touched her earlier.

Touching her own cheek and smiling, maybe they could make this work. It wouldn't be easy, but it was worth a try, wasn't it?

After a long while, with Christina growing very impatient and still no sign of Stefano, Sophie decided to go looking for him. Maybe he needed help with the picnic stuff, plus somebody needed to tell him that you never leave children waiting.

Heading down the stairs she heard raised voices, Stefano's being the loudest.

She decided to stay back out of sight and listen, when she realized one of the voices was that of a woman.

Unfortunately, the voices quickly died down and when she heard the door opening of what she assumed must be his home office, she quickly stepped back up to the landing, ever so slightly leaning over the banister to try and get a look at who was coming out.

Stefano came out first, striding purposefully towards the front door and in his wake at a much slower pace, the most beautiful woman she had ever seen. She was tall, slim but shapely in all the right places, wearing white cropped trousers teamed with a simple black tank top and black killer heels, she certainly knew how to dress to emphasize her shape.

As if sensing another woman was in the house, she looked up, pursing her lips in an ugly smirk upon seeing Sophie.

Upon reaching the door Stefano now held open, she delicately touched his arm saying, "See you later, babe," before walking out.

She had seen enough, her stomach felt like it had just exploded inside her own body, running to the bathroom just in time to kneel down and empty the contents of her stomach into the loo.

Resting her head on her arms which were still resting on the toilet seat, she couldn't stop the tears that followed.

She should have trusted her instincts as well as her own eyes. She saw the god damned messages on his phone for crying out loud that very morning.

She was mad to think that he was still interested in her. It had been years. Of course he had moved on and why would he want her when he had a girlfriend like that!

And the look that woman gave her! Of course she would give her a look like that, she would do the same if she found out her boyfriend had a kid and he decided to move them both in. It was probably what they were arguing about.

A knock on the bathroom door had her head snapping up, "Sophie, are you in there?"

Oh, shit it was him, and double shit when she heard Christina's voice calling out, "mummmmy, come on, it's picnic time."

This was the last thing she needed right now, a bloody picnic!

She had already decided before throwing up that she wasn't going anywhere with that two-timing bastard, but she couldn't exactly prevent Christina from going, nor did she want to. Who was she to destroy her daughter's happiness? He would do that all by himself soon enough.

Wiping her tears with her hands, she stood up, "You two go, I don't feel too good."

"Mummy, are you sick?"

The sound of worry in her daughter's voice only made her sick again. The last thing she wanted to do was worry her.

"Mummy's ok darling, it's just a bug."

"Are you sure? Do you want me to call the doctor?" Stefano asked, most probably pretending to care, for Christina's benefit, she thought bitterly.

Walking over to the mirror and wiping her mouth and face, was this going to be her life from now on? she wondered. Hiding away and being sick every time she saw him with another woman? And would he really subject her to such torment after everything they had been through? Maybe, his girlfriend coming over today wasn't planned, it certainly didn't sound like it. Maybe he would go to hers from now on, I mean he couldn't exactly risk Christina bumping into her now, could he?

But every time he would go out, she would know.

She had to mentally detach herself from him but how could she achieve that when her heart cried out to him.

What was that old saying her mum used to say? Oh yeah, "love is like a pile of shit and fool be he who trips and falls in it!" how very true, she thought.

"I'll be fine," she said, more to herself than him.

"Would you like me to get Eleni?"

"I said I'll be fine," she said a little louder this time, why couldn't he just leave her alone?

"Well, we can leave the picnic for later on, maybe you'll feel better later," he suggested.

He didn't want her missing out, they had such a good time this afternoon.

She heard Christina moan out a 'nooo,' to that suggestion, she had been so excited about that picnic. The only picnics she got to enjoy until now were on the living room floor with her and Susan, as the local parks in their area were not nice places to have a picnic in.

"I said I'll be fine, just go and have fun." And not being able to help herself, she added, "Christina has waited long enough."

God knew what he thought of her last remark, but he didn't reply straight away and when he did, he simply said, "Ok, if you need anything Eleni is downstairs. And if you feel better, you know where we'll be."

And off they went as she could hear Christina's voice growing more distant.

When she was sure they were completely gone, she left the bathroom and collapsed on to the bed. The first thought she had was to call Susan but seeing the time and knowing the time difference between Cyprus and the UK, she knew Susan was probably still at work, that phone call would have to wait.

Hearing Christina's voice outside, she went to the balcony doors and looked out, seeing them settled on a red blanket on the beach, with Christina looking busy trying to see how many grapes she could stuff in his mouth.

Hope he chokes on them, she thought and instantly regretted thinking it, he was still Christina's father.

She suddenly felt sad, plain and simple, she felt the sadness to the very depths of her soul.

And let's not forget, she was absolutely fuming with him, how dare he sleep with her and make her think that something was still there between them, why bloody touch her cheek in that way earlier and again last night if he didn't feel anything?

Well, she could easily answer that one, men tend to think with their cocks rather than their heads or hearts, not that this particular man had much of a heart anyway.

How could someone change so much! He used to be her everything, her superman, her whole world and look what had become of them.

If that woman wanted Stefano, then she could have him. She wasn't going to play any games with him, she had her daughter to think of.

Which made her think, what now? Well, one thing was for sure, they were no longer going to share a room, never mind a bed!

She would sleep with Christina and if he didn't like it, then tough shit! It was either that or they were moving out.

She wasn't going to let him blackmail her into sharing his bed nor was she about to let him have his cake and eat it, in this case two cakes.

By the time they came back from the picnic, she had already had her clothes out of his wardrobe and back in her bags ready to move them into Christina's room.

She was just coming out of the bathroom after collecting some more of her things when Stefano came into the room.

Seeing her packed bags, he closed the door behind him, what the hell was going on here? She was supposed to be sick!

"What's going on?" he asked, confused. He thought earlier that they had finally turned a corner but then he walks in on this.

"You tell me," she said, putting her bag of toiletries along with her other things.

"What's that supposed to mean? Tell you what?" From the look on her face, she was fuming, and he had no idea why. Fair enough, the circumstances of her coming here were not ideal but today had felt good between them.

Snorting, "You know what." Did he really think she was that stupid? He obviously spent too much time with bimbos.

"Well, obviously I don't! So why don't you enlighten me?" crossing his arms over his chest.

What on earth was going on here, one minute they're all having fun, the next she's sick and the next she's bloody pissed at God knows what!

He really didn't have the patience for this, especially today, dealing with one crazy woman today was more than enough.

"Your arrogance knows no bounds, you know that."

"So, I've been told."

Picking up her bag and moving towards the door where Stefano still stood not moving a muscle.

"Move."

"I'm not moving anywhere, agami mou, not until you tell me what the hell is going on here, and while you're at it I suggest you watch your tone."

"I'm not your love, you don't get to call me that!" she was definitely raising her voice now, but she didn't care, how dare he tell her to watch her tone, who the hell did he think he was?

"And I will not be sharing a room, a bed with you when you're sleeping with another woman."

Another woman? He couldn't hold it in, he burst into a roaring laugh.

"You think it's funny? Of course you do, what am I saying? This is after all, you we're talking about, isn't it?" adding "By the way, that's a nice message you're sending your daughter."

"ENOUGH!" This time he was the one to raise his voice. He stopped finding her madness funny the instant she mentioned their daughter. She had gone too far with that comment.

"Oh, don't act like you're bothered," staring at him in disgust.

"Oh, agami mou, I'm getting very bothered." Pushing himself from the door and taking a step towards her, "So I suggest you put that bag down and come to your senses quickly because my patience is wearing thin." Running a finger down her bare arm.

His touch instantly raised goosebumps on her skin which didn't go by unnoticed by him if his smirk was anything to go by.

Swallowing down that pesky lump that always had the habit of forming every time he was near, she said with a slightly shaky voice this time, "Oh, my senses are just fine, especially my eyes and ears." Seeing his eyes narrowing, "Yeah, that's right, I saw you earlier."

"You saw what, exactly?" he really didn't have the patience for this, women didn't tend to behave this way towards him. The only woman who ever argued with him was this woman in front of him now but that was a long time ago and never on this level on the madness scale.

"I saw and heard you both."

Ahhh, so that's where this was going, she was jealous.

That thought alone was enough to make him grow hard, because if she was jealous, it meant she still wanted him, like he wanted her.

"And I'll repeat my question, you saw what exactly?"

"Don't play your stupid games with me, go play them with your bimbo." Looking him square in the eyes, "Now move."

Now he was starting to get mad, "No," he said. He wasn't about to let her accuse him of cheating, if indeed that was what she was implying and just walk away.

"Fine."

Dropping her bag, she started to march towards the balcony doors. Well, if she couldn't get out through one door then she'll get out through the other.

Before she could even lay a finger on the handle, Stefano grabbed her by the arm and spun her round, pushing her back against the doors, caging her in with his hands against the door on either side of her head.

"And how exactly are you planning on escaping? Because unless you plan on flying out of here, you're not going anywhere, agami mou." Leaning forward and adding the agami mou against her ear.

Well, he had a point there, she thought. She hadn't quite planned on what to do once on the balcony.

Seeing the smugness on his face, she knew he knew he got her there and it only served to infuriate her even more. She just wanted to smack that look off his face.

Putting her hands against his chest, she pushed as hard as she could.

"Get away from me." She yelled, but she might as well be pushing against a brick wall.

Grabbing her by both arms and holding her tight, "Get a grip, Sophie, you're being irrational."

Trying to pull out of his grip was pretty useless considering she was trapped between him in front and the balcony door on her back, but she didn't let that stop her from trying, pulling and twisting to get away from him.

Not because she was afraid of him but more because she was afraid of herself and what she might do.

Seeing him with that woman today made her realize that she was still in love with him, to say she was mad with envy was a major understatement. She wanted to rip that woman's hair out by the roots and well, literally batter her, if she was deadly honest with herself.

Pinning her arms above her head and holding them in place by one hand, he grabbed her chin with the other, it wasn't with too much force but just enough to get her to stop fighting and look at him.

He could see the defiant look in her eyes even as he had her in this position, Sophie was never one to give up. It was one of the things he loved about her amongst many others - she was the strongest, bravest woman he had ever known. To move countries, start afresh and have a baby all by herself; he was in awe of her.

He was standing so close to her that with every heaving breath she took, her breasts gently grazed against him making him instantly hard.

Looking from her eyes to her mouth he couldn't help slowly running his thumb along her lower lip. When she closed her eyes and he saw her lip tremble, that was his breaking point.

Tightening his grip on her chin, he took her mouth in a long hard kiss, when she responded by opening her mouth, he pushed past her lips with his tongue to delve deeper inside the warmth of her mouth, tasting her, savouring her, making her head swirl with desire.

She wanted to wrap her arms around his neck but when she tried to move her arms he just held on tighter, not letting her go.

She knew she shouldn't, she was supposed to be angry with him, but she couldn't help the way her body was reacting to him. Her body was betraying her mind but was it betraying her heart?

She felt an ache in her belly and a throbbing between her legs, she found herself pressing her body hard against him in a desperate attempt to ease her discomfort.

He could feel her breasts crushed against him, taking his hand from her chin he slid it down to capture her breast, grazing his thumb against her nipple which was so hard it was straining against her clothes.

Leaving her lips, he trailed a line of kisses down her slender neck then licking his way back up, making her tremble.

Capturing her mouth with his, she felt him undo the single button on her denim shorts and place his hand between her legs.

Slipping his finger inside her knickers, he stroked and caressed before slipping that finger deep inside making her gasp against his mouth and squeeze her legs shut over his hand, to keep it there.

She was so hot and wet, he just wanted to bury himself deep inside her and never come out.

Without breaking off the kiss, he released her hands, eased his finger out and pulled down her shorts along with her knickers which Sophie quickly stepped out of.

Wrapping her arms around his neck and bringing her body closer, he placed his hands beneath her buttocks and lifted her up.

With her legs wrapped firmly around his waist, she could feel his thick hard length straining against his trousers.

With one hand he quickly undid his zipper, setting himself free. Pushing her back against the door he finally plunged into her deep and hard again and again, driving them both to new heights.

He could feel her arms tightening around his neck, her quick little gasps against his neck.

She felt so damn good wrapped around him, he couldn't hold on much longer, he needed her to come with him, she was so close he could feel her.

Reaching down between them with one hand he rubbed and pressed against her clit with his thumb making her pant and moan against him.

He pushed forward harder and faster while increasing the tempo with his thumb making her scream out and convulse all around him.

The feel of her muscles tightening around him was enough to set him on fire as he erupted deep inside her.

Chapter 8

Six weeks had gone by since he found Sophie and Christina and it's been five weeks and three days since they last spoke to each other, but who was counting?

Thankfully it seemed Christina was oblivious to what was going on with her parents, bringing the saying 'ignorance is bliss,' to mind.

He spent most of his mornings at work, then back home spending his afternoons with his daughter, either playing in the playroom or going to the beach.

He quickly found out that she wasn't exaggerating when she said she didn't know how to swim so he had made sure they dedicated some time for swimming lessons, alongside building numerous sandcastles.

The evenings consisted of them all having dinner outside on the terrace with Christina busy chatting away to Eleni and Costa about her day and not noticing that her mother and father weren't even talking to each other.

They had both decided that it was best for Christina not to realize what was going on between them, for her sake, so Sophie agreed to put her clothes back and stay in the room.

He in turn decided it was best to give her some space and would spend his evenings in his home office catching up on some paperwork which he had neglected lately, partly due to the fact that he spent all his afternoons playing with Christina.

But his daughter came first and always would, he had a lot of time to make up for.

When it was late enough and he knew she would be sleeping, he would quietly sneak up to their room and get into bed beside her, often lying on his side watching her sleep; it was the only time he could admire her without her giving him dirty looks.

It was so hard living in the same house, sleeping in the same bed with her and not actually being with her; it was a sad imitation of their past.

But he was happy just having her here even if she didn't speak to him. Give it time, he told himself, she would come round.

Waking up in the morning and seeing him fast asleep beside her in bed for the first time in weeks actually startled her.

Of course she knew he was sleeping in the bed at night, only because the sheets were always crinkled on his side, but he always came to bed after she had fallen asleep and would always be gone before she woke up.

He felt like a ghost, always there but never seen. The only time she actually laid eyes on him was during dinner, but she would never dream of trying to speak to him in front of Christina, Eleni and Costa, partly because she didn't want to be humiliated if he ended up ignoring her.

She knew she had hurt him when she accused him of cheating and for that she was sorry, if she could take it back, she would, but she couldn't.

So, she decided to give him some space, hoping that would magically heal the distance between them. How ironic she thought, hoping to heal distance with distance, foolish more like!

After they had sex that day, Stefano immediately became withdrawn with her which wasn't what she had expected to happen but seriously what did she expect? Cuddles in bed? After the things she had said to him? Come on!

After pulling up his trousers, which he did much quicker than her, by the way, due to the fact that he didn't step out of them, while she just pulled up hers and had to abandon doing her button to catch the phone he threw at her and asked, no, not asked, that was too mild, more like demanded she read the messages he received from that woman, all the while standing there in front of her with his arms crossed watching her.

Of course, she had already seen the messages that very morning but upon seeing them again, it was like seeing them for the first time.

What she actually didn't realize the first time was that Stefano never replied to any of those messages and when reading them again out loud, at Stefano's insistence, realized how begging they sounded.

He explained that they had only dated for a short while and upon her question of how long that short while actually was, she found out that it was only a few weeks, maybe a couple of months max and he had broken up with her a few days before going to London.

She had realized her mistake at that point, but it was too late, the damage had been done. Stefano wasn't a man who believed in giving second chances, his father had given her father a chance many years ago and it nearly ruined his family's business. He probably thought betrayal was a family trait. She wouldn't blame him if he never spoke to her again.

Focusing back to the present and at the man fast asleep beside her, tears suddenly welled up and threatened to fall.

She reached out her hand to touch his cheek but decided against it, it hurt too damn much to be this close to him but not close enough.

What had become of them? She asked herself in disbelief.

They were so close once; one couldn't breathe without the other and they turned into this!

What if she didn't leave the country? What if he didn't listen to her father? What if she told him she was pregnant? There were a lot of ifs and unfortunately, they would never know the answers.

Getting slowly out of bed and getting dressed in the bathroom so as not to wake him, she went to get Christina ready for the day.

Usually, he was up and gone by the time she even woke up, not wanting to make her uncomfortable by finding him beside her, but this morning he found himself waking up late and Sophie was gone.

Must be all these late nights and early starts he was having; always the last one down and the first one up, that would take a toll on anyone's body.

Touching the sheet on her side of the bed, he realized it was cold, which meant she had been up for a while. It was stupid really, but he found himself almost feeling guilty for her finding him in bed.

He shook his head to try and shake away the irrational feeling and decided to get up.

Deciding to work from home today, he pulled on his grey jogging bottoms and white t-shirt and decided to go downstairs for some coffee. He really needed Eleni's strong Greek coffee this morning.

As he headed down the stairs, he could already hear Christina's excited bubbly voice. When he reached the kitchen what he saw stopped him from going in straight away; it was truly a sight to behold - what he had always imagined having a family with Sophie would look like.

That didn't mean he was old fashioned and believed a woman's place was in the kitchen by any means, but only because he knew Sophie's love for baking.

There was Sophie, Eleni and little Christina, standing on a foot stool in the middle, making traditional Cypriot breadsticks, which happened to be his favourite.

Sophie used to make them for him every weekend back then and no one could ever make them as good as she did. Eleni made them all the time, but they just weren't the same and he didn't have the heart to tell her that.

He could stand here and watch them like this all day - Sophie rolling out the dough and Christina patting the sesame seeds on to them and almost flattening them.

It was Eleni who happened to look up and see him standing in the open doorway, ending the hypnotic sensation.

"My son, come in," she said, motioning for him to come in and take a seat.

Sophie looked up from what she was doing and stood up from where she was sitting on the bar stool.

One look at her face told him to run towards her as she suddenly collapsed backwards, reaching her just in time to hear the sound her head made when hitting the tiles but not in time to prevent it, almost made him physically sick.

Instantly the kitchen filled up with panicked cries - Christina crying out for her mummy, Eleni crying out 'banayiamou' and calling out for her husband and all the while he was trying to remain calm for Sophie.

"Sophie? Sophie?" he called, but no answer.

She was so white, he placed his hand underneath her head to try and move her but when he did, he realized his hand was wet and sticky. Pulling his hand back and almost too afraid to look, he saw it was coated in blood. She must have cracked her head when she fell.

"Should I call an ambulance, Stefano?" Eleni asked.

"No, I'll take her. It'll be quicker."

Cyprus had some of the best doctors, especially if you were private, but the ambulance service in the country was one of the worst in the world. He could almost imagine them finishing off their coffee before deciding if they should answer an emergency call.

Lifting her up in his arms, he quickly carried her to his car.

Waking up in a bright white room, her head was throbbing in pain, so much so that she turned her head to the side to vomit.

When she was done, she realized someone was beside her holding a kidney dish which she had thankfully puked up in and not on herself. Looking up she saw it was Stefano, concern clearly on his face.

"Hey, how are you feeling?" he asked.

Taking a few deep breaths and massaging her temples to ease the pain and nausea, "What happened," she asked.

The last thing she remembered was being in the kitchen making breadsticks with Christina and Eleni and now she was here. Which by the way, where was here? Was she in hospital?

"Am I in hospital?" she asked him this time.

"Yes. You fainted and when you landed you cracked your head on the tiles in the kitchen. I'm sorry I didn't get to you in time."

He sounded sincere when he said that last part, but she didn't have the strength to think about what that might mean right now.

She touched the back of her head and winced at the pain, feeling sick again.

"Sophie, have you been taking your heart medication?" he asked gently, a lot had happened lately, and he wouldn't have blamed her if she'd forgotten.

"Yes, I think so." She couldn't remember or even think clearly.

"You think so?"

"Yeah, I have," she said, shaking her head.

She didn't seem too sure but she was starting to turn white again so he decided to just wait for the doctor to come back and hopefully they would have some answers then.

"Ok, you rest agapi mou, we'll see what the doctor says when he gets back." Looking at his watch, "it shouldn't be too long now, he said they'll have the results in an hour."

Seeing her look down at the plaster on the inside of her elbow, "They took some bloods," he said, quietly, he knew she was afraid of needles.

"Thank god I was passed out," she said and laid back down closing her eyes, which was a bad idea as the second she did, it felt like she was spinning out of control on a merry go round and falling down into a deep black hole.

Lifting her head again and puking in the dish Stefano held out for her with one hand and held her hair back with the other.

At that moment the doctor came into the room, "Ah, you're awake Sophia mou. How are you feeling?"

"Sick." She said, lifting up her head and wiping her mouth with a tissue Stefano handed her, while he was mopping her brow with a cool cloth.

"We'll give you some anti-sickness for that, but I'm here to discuss your blood results and to examine you again."

"Again? Why? You said the injury to her head was only superficial. Is it to do with her heart?"

"No no Stefano, her heart is fine and so is her head." Looking at Sophie "You'll have a headache for a few days, it was quite a bump you took but you'll be fine," he said, smiling.

"Then what is it, doctor?" Stefano asked, putting down the face cloth he was holding and taking hold of her hand instead.

In that moment, seeing the look of concern on his face and the way he was looking after her she thought she could see the old Stefano. Maybe he was still in there after all.

"Sophia, your blood results have detected the pregnancy hormone."

"What?" Sophie and Stefano both said at the same time.

Looking from Sophie to Stefano and back again, "But, of course, we can't be one hundred percent sure until we do a scan. Do I have your permission to do that now?" he asked.

"Erm, yeah, of course."

Looking over at Stefano she caught him straightening up and swallowing down hard. In that moment her heart shattered in to a million pieces, not again, she thought.

From the look of pure panic on his face and the way he kept on swallowing like he had a golf ball stuck in his throat, she would take a wild guess and say he didn't want another kid.

Oh, he loved Christina, she would never deny that but it didn't mean he wanted another one, with her!

The doctor came back in after leaving the room to get the scan machine.

Two minutes later and it was confirmed, she was six weeks pregnant!

The doctor left the room to go get the anti-sickness medication and to give them some time to process this new information.

Stefano was standing by her side staring at the image on the machine.

After what seemed like hours but, in reality, was only a couple of minutes, she decided to clear her throat a little too loudly just to break the silence in the room and also because she didn't have the faintest idea of what to say.

"Where is it?" he asked, pointing at the scan.

Of all the things she thought he might say, that was not one of them.

"Erm, I'm not really sure to be honest, it's so small right now."

When he didn't say anything and continued to just stare at the screen, she decided to speak first. She needed to know where she stood, there was no way in hell she was going to let history repeat itself. She might have got lucky and pulled it off with one kid but two, now that was a different story.

She couldn't raise two kids on her own.

"Stefano, I know this isn't ideal. I know you don't want another baby..."

Before she could finish her sentence, Stefano looked at her, "Is that what you think?" he asked frowning.

"Isn't it?"

"No, it's not. I always wanted and still do want lots of children..."

"Just not with me."

"With you! It was always you. I want my own football team, with you."

Taking both her hands in his, and sitting down in the chair by her bed, "But I'm scared," he confessed.

"Of what?" Stefano scared? She couldn't imagine this man ever being scared, of anything.

"Of losing you," he said with a voice close to cracking.

"After your last experience and the heart condition you mentioned, what if it's too much pressure on your heart and I lose you. We have to think about this, I can't lose you again. At least back then I knew you were still in the world. If anything happens to you, I won't be able to go on without you."

For the first time she could see tears in his eyes.

She couldn't help it, she reached out and placed a hand on his cheek.

"If I have to choose, I choose you, agami mou." A tear falling down onto her hand.

He continued, "There was a dream, and I say 'was' because the day you came back into my life with Christina, it stopped! But that dream haunted me every single night I went to sleep since the day your father came to see me."

He stopped talking, to take a deep breath and she just watched, bringing her hand up to take hold of his in hers, silently urging him on, feeling like this was something he had to get out.

Swallowing down hard, "It was the same every night, it was always dark, cloudy and raining and I look down at my right hand," looking down at his hand in hers, "and I see the tiniest baby there. So tiny it's lying on its back on the palm of my hand and I'm walking down the street looking for its mother. Everyone's in such a hurry to get out of the rain, that no one stops to give us a second look, to help me, and then I suddenly realise that something's not right with the baby. It's too small, babies shouldn't be that small, and it's not crying, not moving, and that's when I realise the truth, the baby's dead. And that's when I wake up."

Looking up at her, bringing their hands up and kissing her knuckles, "That was you, the mother I was looking for in the dream, it was you."

She didn't realize she was crying until he reached out and wiped one of her tears away with his thumb, her heart ached for him. This whole time she thought she was the only one who was wronged, who suffered, but as it turned out, he suffered just as much as she did, possibly more.

Leaning her cheek into the palm of his hand, she realized that in that moment everything that happened between them recently was forgotten. He loved her, he always did, she knew that now and she loved him, always had.

They both deserved the future that was rightfully theirs.

Chapter 9

Lying on the surgical table with Stefano right beside her holding their baby boy in his arms, it was one of the happiest moments of her life.

The first being the day she had Christina and the second was her and Stefano's wedding day six months ago. Amidst all the hectic chaos of Stefano opening a new hotel in London and Sophie opening her very own bakery they had decided on a quick wedding, because in Stefano's own words he wanted to tie her to him before she changed her mind and for her because she didn't want to be too fat in her wedding dress. She was only going to do this once, so might as well look hot! Right?

Stefano flew his brother over from London to conduct their ceremony and with him came Susan, who, of course, was maid of honor.

But one of the biggest surprises of all, that day, was when her mother turned up at the church just before the wedding was to take place.

The instant she saw her mother she had run in to her open arms and stayed there until Christina came and pulled on her dress asking why she was crying, which unashamedly she didn't realize she was sobbing like a child.

She went on to introduce Christina to her grandmother, at which point it was her mother's turn to start crying; obviously happy tears but Sophie knew deep down that they were also guilty tears.

She didn't blame her mother; she only did what she did because she was afraid of her husband.

But things were going to be different from now on, she was back!

And the third was today, seeing Stefano holding his newborn son.

It was a scary nine months, she wasn't going to lie, she ended up suffering from that severe form of sickness, hyperemesis gravidarum, their doctor called it, which made it extremely difficult to keep anything down. Her pregnancy with Christina was plain sailing compared to this one. There were days when she truly felt like she had been poisoned, and not a day went by that she didn't thank her lucky stars that she had Stefano by her side because she honestly didn't know how she would have survived that without him. That said, there were times when the fear would really take over both of them, but their doctor had assured them both that as long as she had a C-section and not a natural birth and took all her medication, she would be fine.

And here she was, to tell the tale.

She couldn't wait to go home and show Christina her baby brother.

"I love you," she said to her husband, looking up at him holding their son.

"I love you too," giving her a long, tender kiss.

Looking over at the doctor, "Hey doc, how long, until we can try for the third?"

CPSIA information can be obtained
at www.ICGtesting.com
Printed in the USA
BVHW081950131221
623939BV00013B/516

9 781915 164230